Rainbow's
Tide

Raider's Tide

MAGGIE PRINCE

An imprint of HarperCollinsPublishers

My warmest thanks for items of historical information go to
Chris Groenewald, David Pile, Lindsay Warden,
Susan Wilson of Lancaster Reference Library and Local History Archive,
Andrew White of Lancaster Museum Services,
Andrew Thynne of Preston Public Records Office,
the staff of Kendal Library and Senate House Library
and to my sister Phyllis, for help in updating my writing technology.

First published in Great Britain by Collins in 2002
Collins is an imprint of HarperCollins*Publishers* Ltd
77-85 Fulham Palace Road, Hammersmith, London W6 8JB

The HarperCollins website address is www.**fire**and**water**.com

1 3 5 7 9 8 6 4 2

ISBN 000 712403 1

Printed and bound in Great Britain by
Omnia Books Limited, Glasgow

For Chris, Deborah, Daniel,
and for my mother whose
landscape this is, with
love and thanks.

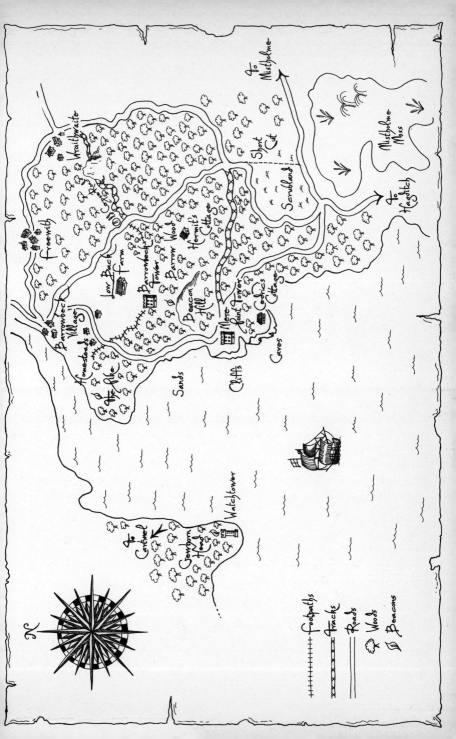

The northern counties from time to time had to withstand invasion by the organised forces of Scotland, but their chief embarrassment was caused by a system of predatory incursions which rendered life and property insecure.

Victoria County History of Cumberland

They have taken forth of divers families all, the very rackencrocks and pot-hooks. They have driven away all the beasts, sheep and horses...

The Silver Dale, by William Riley

On 14 April... the Scots did come... armed and appointed with gavlockes and crowes of iron, handpeckes, axes and skailinge lathers.

Border Papers, Scottish Records ii 171

*In transposing Beatrice's story into modern English,
the tone and content of her original narrative
have been preserved throughout,
and her exact words wherever possible.*

It is the late 1500s. Queen Elizabeth I is on the throne of England...

Chapter 1

I jump up, jolted out of my daydream. I thought I heard voices, muttering secretively. I peer into the dimness of the woods and listen. It's easy to start imagining things when you're alone on the last watch of the day. On the other hand, my hearing is sharp – sharper than average – and I often hear what I am not supposed to.

I rest my hand on the haft of my knife, and creep through the swathes of pale cream daffodils to where the rough ground of the Pike slopes down towards the sea. My knife has worn through the bottom of its sheath, and keeps catching on my skirts. I shift it round to the back of me, and move out into the open where the warning beacon stands, a pile of sticks and turf in a stone trough. I can see nothing out of the ordinary, just the sun going down in the west, shining red through the beacon's propped twigs.

We keep watch because of a very real danger. It is three years since we were last attacked by Scottish raiders, who creep round the bay in their boats or race out of the hills from the border country. Now it is spring again, the invasion season, and a watch must be kept until the first winter frosts.

The sound isn't repeated. I suppose I'm just jumpy, for I have worse problems than Scots to think of at the moment. Light glints on fast-moving water far below me, and I sit on the edge of the beacon to watch the bore tide coming up the bay. The wind wraps my skirts round my legs and brings fine sand billowing up the slope. I push my hair back under my lace cap, and glance south along the coast to where my cousins' pele tower stands above the sea on its limestone cliffs. The tower itself cannot be seen from here, but warning smoke from their beacon can, when necessary. Yes, there are worse things than Scots. I was sixteen last birthday, and people have begun murmuring about marriage.

This past six years, since I was no longer a child, I have known that I must marry my Cousin Hugh, as my sister must marry his brother, Gerald, to ensure preservation within the family of our two farmsteads. It had always, until now, seemed a safely distant prospect.

I stand up and make a last patrol round the slopes, kicking my way through the bracken, straining my ears for anything that is not part of the normal life of the Pike. There's nothing, just rustlings in the undergrowth as small night creatures wake up, and the distant screaming of seagulls above the tide line. I collect my cloak from a bramble bush and set off downhill through the forest, leaving the sea behind.

It is darker here, but I see it almost at once, a rust-coloured rag hanging from the lower branches of a wych elm. I struggle through the brambles to reach it, sick already. It is warm and motionless, surprisingly solid under its soft fur, a snared squirrel, choked by the wire noose it ran through.

Perhaps this tiny tragedy was what I heard earlier. I loosen the wire and lift it down, sad little hunchback. Its red tail drifts like thistledown against my wrist. Barrowbeck villagers hunt the squirrels for their tails, which make pretty if distressing gown edgings. For a moment I do not feel in any way like a grown woman, old enough to marry. Instead I feel childlike and inadequate, not up to dealing with a world which can do this. I settle the squirrel amongst the roots of the tree and am about to cover it with last year's dead leaves, when it twitches and blinks, then runs up the tree and is gone. It must just have had the breath knocked out of it by the noose. I laugh, relieved, feeling my heart pounding in my throat at the shock, then pick my way back to the steep path. Above me, the squirrel flickers away through the treetops. Below me, my own family's pele tower stands in the valley on its raised shoulder of land, a foursquare limestone fortress. I make my way down the hill, more unnerved than ever now, avoiding tree roots and white rocks that poke like bones through the soil. Behind me, in the darkening woods, one late blackbird sings wildly.

In the valley I pass the stonewalled midden where Leo, our cowman, is shovelling manure. He calls out, "Evening, Mistress Beatrice!" and grins. I wave back. "'Tis a good evening for Scots," he calls after me. I sigh, and lift the heavy iron latch of the gatehouse door. Somehow, I'm not in the mood for Leo's wit tonight.

In the gatehouse I step over the horse rug. I never stand on it. It used to be Peter, my favourite pony. The heat from the candle on the wall-pricket sears my cheek. I leave the door open for a moment to allow fresh air in. This nail-studded door, half the thickness of an oak tree, is the only outer door to our home, and therefore the only entrance to defend when we are attacked, but the result on the lower floors, where there are no windows either, is that the air is often stale and heavy. The only other way out is underground, a passage below the kitchen which leads downhill to the barmkin, the high-walled enclosure where our animals are sometimes kept.

I open the inner door. Greasy smoke hangs in the gloom. I can hear the clank of iron pans beyond the low arch which leads to Kate's kitchen. There will be bread warming on the hearth, and stew steaming in a pot suspended from the rackencrock over the fire. I'm hungry, and Kate will be angry with me for being late, but I need to breathe. This is too suffocating after the wind on the

16

Pike. I set off up the spiral stone staircase, and meet my younger sister, Verity, coming down.

"Beatie, where were you? I'm trying to sort out next week's watch rota. Germaine wants to exchange with you on Monday." She sits down on a step.

Verity at fifteen is taller than me, her hair a darker brown and her eyes a darker blue. The word which older members of the family use to describe her is 'wilful'. Verity really couldn't care less what they say. She is one of the people I am closest to in the world. I sit down on the step below her.

"Sorry. I was on the Pike. Dickon has the ague and there was no lookout, so I took over his watch. Where's Mother?"

"She's out. She went off in a temper to visit Aunt Juniper."

We exchange a look. "And Father?" There are only two places where Father might be: lying in wait next to the highway, or drinking himself into a stupor upstairs.

Verity pulls a face and gestures up the stairs. I groan. Faintly I can hear Germaine playing one of the nauseatingly sentimental tunes my father adores, on her three-stringed fiddle. "I wish I'd stayed on the Pike," I mutter, feeling a twinge of longing for the peace there. Nature might be brutal and complicated, but at least it doesn't play the fiddle.

We talk a little longer about how to organise the watch, then I continue on up four floors, round and round the circling steps, to the battlements. It's turning cold. I pull my hooded cloak more closely round me. In the centre of the battlements is the crenellated beacon turret, with its tall wooden pole topped by an iron crossbar and two tar barrels, ready to be ignited should any neighbouring beacon flare up in warning. We keep a ring of fire here on the coast. There are beacons on the Pike, on Beacon Hill behind us, at my cousins' pele tower along the cliffs and on Gewhorn Head, the promontory across the bay.

Up here on the battlements the air smells of damp earth and new leaves. William, one of my father's henchmen, is on guard tonight. He is dozing on his feet, but when he hears me he jumps, and starts marching dizzyingly round the battlements, his gaze turning from west to north to east.

"Good evening, William."

"Good evening, Mistress Beatrice."

I lean with my elbows on the stone parapet, and after a moment William joins me. Stars are coming out in the east, like maker's flaws in expensive blue pottery. In the west the last glow, as if from a kiln, shows uneasily. Bats dip and swing below us. Far down in the meadow Leo heads home, and a homesteader calls to her dog.

I love all this, but I do not love my Cousin Hugh, except as a cousin. If the queen refuses to marry, why cannot I? I am perfectly capable of running this farm unaided. Verity and I mostly do already. Why, for heaven's sake, would I need a husband?

"Lord Allysson's carriage is coming through tonight," William says in an offhand manner.

I turn to look at him. "Have you told my father?"

His gaze slides away. "I had to, mistress. I didn't want another beating like the last one. Mebbe a sprig of valerian in his wine? I reckon he's got wise to Mistress Verity's trick with the stone in his horse's shoe."

I sigh. "I could try it. Thanks William." It isn't easy having a father who's a part-time highway robber.

Back downstairs in the kitchen Kate, our cook, is standing inside the hearth, stirring something, her hair wrapped in a white cloth and her overskirts tucked into her belt. She lifts her red face from the blaze.

"About time, young woman. This broth is well nigh incinerated. Get your plate." A cauldron of steaming mutton stew is standing on a trivet at the side of the fire. Kate ladles some on to my plate, and takes half a loaf of black bread from the warming oven in the wall. I sit down at the long table, mutter a quick grace and eat in silence. Verity has vanished now, but elsewhere in the tower Germaine's music creaks on.

Kate throws more logs on the fire and turns the wheel of the bellows, sending the flames roaring high. I realise now that she is boiling bones for glue. The disgusting smell starts to fill the kitchen. Kate sings while she works, something about a cold-hearted maiden who condemns a young man to die by not loving him enough. I find that my sympathies lie entirely with the maiden. Kate crosses to the chopping block on its tree-trunk legs, lines up the next batch of mutton bones left over from the stew and swings her cleaver high. The firelight throws her giant shadow across the smoky walls. Our kitchen is the only room which is two storeys high, to dissipate heat and allow some light in, since there are no windows on the ground floor. High up, the narrow window slits show the night sky. Owls and bats live up there. There are flutterings as Kate's shadow flies through the darkness and crashes down. I shiver. There is a strange feeling in the air tonight.

Later, in my room three floors up, I peer out of the window. We had glass put into some of our windows last year – not into the arrow slits of course – and so it is more difficult to see out now, through these tiny, greenish panes. I thought I heard a horse outside, and my father's nervous cough. I do wonder quite how all this expensive glass came to be paid for.

A heated stone lies in my bed, under my sheepskin bedcover. My cat, Caesar, grudgingly relinquishes his place on it as I climb between the sheets. I leave my faded blue bed-curtains open. I don't want to be cut off from the world tonight. When I kick the warmingstone out, scents of lavender and thyme billow up from the rushes on the floor. Caesar sidles on to the stone, jumps back, creeps up on it again. Finally he decides to burn, and his purring is like the sea on the pebbles over the hill as we both settle down for the night.

I dream of Scots. They are in the lower section of the spiral staircase where it opens into the gatehouse and the kitchen archway. I run up the stairs away from them, but it is worse there, because the stairs are enclosed and narrow between curving walls, and I cannot see how close they are behind me.

I wake with a jump, hot and trembling. In the darkness the dream is still too real. I stare in the direction of my door. I am afraid to reach out for my tinderbox and candle, but eventually I do. The shadows swoop and dance as I light the candle. I need company to drive the nightmare away, so I wrap a shawl round my shoulders and go up on to the battlements, throwing glances behind me down the stairs. Martinus is on watch. He smiles and greets me, and talks comfortably of ordinary things, food, horses, the pattern of the stars, and we stand for a long time leaning against the beacon turret, under the stare of the wall-eyed moon.

Chapter 2

In the morning I find that my mother has still not returned, so I decide to walk over the hill to Aunt Juniper's to meet her, and perhaps have another half-hearted go at seeing Hugh in a husbandly light. Before this, however, there are the morning's tasks. We are not rich. We do not have many servants, so Verity and I do much of the work involved in running the household and farm. This morning I set some of the men to pounding seaweed into our outer door, to make it fireproof for the summer. We are late doing it this year. Then I walk down the hill to open the barmkin and release the flock of sheep belonging to our neighbour, James Sorrell. The sunshine drives away the last of my nightmares. I have vague recollections of dreaming about Hugh dressed in a suit of armour, which in view of my misgivings was probably wishful thinking.

This is a good time to be alive. Queen Elizabeth is on the throne and stability reigns throughout the land. We hear of distant battles fought and won by our English army and navy on land and sea, the news sometimes brought to us a year or more after they happened by fancy-talking travellers from the south. Our only real problem is the Scots, who raid the border counties of Westmorland, Cumberland and Northumberland from March to September every year, though I daresay they feel that we are their problem too, since our men also cross the border from time to time.

There's a lot to do now that spring is here. Our lower rooms and cellars, which have been used as food stores through the winter, must now be cleared, so that cattle, goats and horses can be herded in there fast in the event of a raid. There are times when I wish that one or both of my parents took more interest in the daily running of Barrowbeck Tower.

My father appears to be limping this morning, and I wonder if last night's robbery on the highway did not go according to plan. "Hurt your leg, Father?" Verity asks unsympathetically as she sorts stones to repair the barmkin wall. Father is tottering down the slope towards the dairy in search of fresh milk for his morning dish of bread and milk. Despite their mutual insults it is always obvious how fond Verity and Father are of each other. I think they recognise themselves in each other. I am more like Mother, full of dreams and secrets.

"You can give back yon good pair of shoes if you don't like what bought 'em, Daughter," he shouts at her. Verity takes off her shoes and throws them at his retreating back, but he ignores them. I hold the barmkin gate open for him, and he shambles in, pushing his way among the sheep who are shambling out.

James's sheep have been kept overnight in our barmkin instead of on their normal grazing on the saltmarsh foreshore, because it was full moon last night, and they would have been caught by the high tide, as has happened to many a human soul. I watch the sheep go strolling off down the hill on each other's heels like, well, sheep, and I head back up to the tower. We all have to come and go to and from the barmkin the long way round. From outside it appears a separate thing from the tower. It is a high-walled, semi-circular enclosure lower down the hill, attached at each end to the sheer rockface from which our impregnable outer wall rises. The Scots have breached the barmkin many times, but they have never found the secret stone archway hidden under the floor of the dairy, which itself is built straight into the rock wall, like a cave. Deep in the hill an underground passage leads to our storage cellars and the curving slope up to the kitchen. Even if they did ever find it, they would then be confronted by an iron-bound oak door and a spiked wolf-pit. We scarcely ever come and go this way, for fear of leaving marks of passage, though the temptation is often great on a rainy day.

By midday Mother still has not returned, so I set off to walk up through Barrow Wood and over Beacon Hill to meet her. I want to talk to her alone. Nothing is inevitable. No official betrothal has taken place between Hugh and me. Not even the preliminary *de futuro* contract has been signed. I need to catch her in a good mood and make my case. She and my father are a glowing example of why matrimony should be avoided. She has often told the story of how, as a bride of sixteen, she travelled the Old Corpse Road on the back of a donkey to marry my father. "It would have been better had I married the donkey," she once said in an unguarded moment.

Saint Hilda, my horse, is cropping thistles at the edge of the trees as I enter Barrow Wood. I stroke her nose and decide to leave her behind today. Walking will allow me more time for thought. I have a good nuncheon of cheese and bread in my sheepskin bag. I do not intend to hurry back.

I follow the direct but strenuous route over the top of the hill, where flat, fissured limestone slabs alternate with patches of bracken. Herb Robert grows in crevices, and lady's-slipper orchids tremble in the shade. I take off my boots. The stones are warm and smooth through my black linen stockings. I sit down on a rock to eat, looking out over the bay.

This is not my best batch of bread ever. It emerged from the oven dark and bitter-tasting. I fear there was a mould in last year's wheat, caused by the damp spring.

Sometimes these moulds cause outbreaks of madness right across the north of England. We've tried all ways to keep the bitterness out of the bread, such as not letting the leaven stand too long, a week instead of a fortnight. Unfortunately, the resulting bread is then so hard that you could brain Scots with it.

The mould tends to be worse in the barley and rye bread which the homesteaders make. I wonder sometimes how far the death-hunts and burnings which sometimes plague us round here are a result of these outbreaks of collective madness.

The beacon is behind me, a raised stone hearth piled with wood and turf. I lean my back against it. A tinderbox lies in a covered cavity beneath it, with dried moss and tar-soaked rotten sticks for kindling. I gaze round me, sleepy in the warmth and stillness. The crown of the hill is like a monk's skull, a white summit fringed by trees. There are still monks over the water at Cartmel, despite the old king's wisdom in tearing down their dens of iniquity. Sometimes I wonder about the iniquity. Despite being impoverished themselves, the Cartmel monks give to the poor, and are also said to shelter fugitives.

I look out across the distant curve of the bay to Gewhorn Head, where wolves still roam occasionally, and beyond, to the lakeland hills hidden in a smudge of mist. This is when James Sorrell appears. I don't know which of us receives the bigger fright when his face materialises above the rock wall.

"Beatie, whatever are you doing here?"

"I'm on my way to meet my mother, James. For heaven's sake, how do you manage to be so quiet? You frightened the life out of me. What are you doing here?"

"It's my turn on watch." He sits down beside me, and looks at me in silence. James does not communicate well. His manners are often rough, and surprisingly for a landed farmer in our prosperous region of the north, he has never learned to read or write. I feel it is something to do with the fact that his father used to beat him half senseless when he was a child. We all knew it. I can remember my mother flying into a rage with the old man, and being shown briskly off the premises of Low Back Farm. Because James cannot read or write, Verity keeps his farm's financial books for him, and as a result he has fallen in love with her.

He takes off his leather jerkin. He smells of sweat and cattle. "I haven't seen Verity lately," he says. For some reason, perhaps because he knows I like him, James lives in the forlorn hope that I will help him obtain my fifteen-year-old sister's hand in marriage. Nothing could be further from my mind.

"She's busy, James," I answer, and pass him some bread and cheese to cheer him up. We sit in silence for a while. The world is very beautiful today. Below the rocky plateau on which we sit, on a level with our feet, young hazel leaves are curling out of their buds. High above us a hawk hovers. Trouble for someone. A hint of the strange feeling

I had yesterday returns. I say, "You know, James, I feel as if we're being watched."

"Aye?" He looks sceptical. "It'll be the Green Man, I daresay."

I laugh. Now he is making me nervous. "*No*, nothing like that. I expect it's just a deer watching us from the woods."

He smiles. "Well it'll be the Green Man now. Speak and ye'll see."

"Oh stop it, James." I lean back, knowing he finds it amusing to frighten people, and wishing I had not started this conversation and given him the opportunity. There's nothing on this sunlit hill to harm us. Except – a flicker of light westwards across the bay. I straighten and stare. James has seen it too. He sits forward. The flicker vanishes and is replaced by a thin line of smoke rising from the watchtower across the water. It is the warning beacon. The Scots are coming.

Chapter 3

I have a moment of simply not believing it. I think, this doesn't happen. Three years without a raid have made me complacent.

It makes me slow, slow to react, slow to get on my feet and grapple the tinderbox from its dry place under the beacon. James is faster. He is flinging dried moss and tarry sticks on to the pyre, poking them under the wood, pinching out little tendrils for me to light. I strike a shower of sparks into the moss. All of them go out. I strike again. A few sparks wriggle along the dry filaments and then they go out too. I strike again. The moss takes, bursts into flame. I light one of the tarry sticks from it, twisting it, giving it air, and then thrust it into the centre. A fragile line of smoke trails upwards. James picks up his jerkin and sways it back and forth to create a draught, not too hard, not too gently. He is good with fires. With a sigh, a rotten branch catches and sends up a puff of flame.

"Best run now," says James.

I pull on my boots and ram the tinderbox back into its hole, then follow James across the clearing. We pick up speed when we leave the summit with its ankle-twisting fissures, and start a slithering rush downhill, leaving the path and taking the most direct route. Bracken and tiny treelets whip our ankles. We blunder between ash, hazel and juniper. Behind us the fire burns noisily. I stop and look back, and see the pointed flame flashing high then dipping low, surrounded by a black stream of smoke, shocking against the spring sky.

All I can think is, where are the Scots? Are they coming across the bay at this moment? Are they here already, between me and the safety of the tower? They have been known to hide in the woods for days in some remoter parts, while villagers have gone about their business unawares. James and I both need to round up our livestock. We cannot take losses on the scale of three years ago, particularly as at the tower we have less gold and silver stored in the root cellar for buying new animals this year.

In a good year, Verity goes to market in Lancaster in May with a bag of gold to buy cattle, and to Kendal in August with a bag of silver to buy sheep. I swear the other farmers and auctioneers are more afraid of her than they are of many a grown man. She controls our finances as well as James's. She pays the men, oversees the weighing of the harvest, and, once, the thrashing of a farmhand who stole a bushel of wheat. Only once, because afterwards, as they untied the lad from the elder tree by the barmkin gate, she came into my room, sat down and headed a page in her accounts book *Thefts*. After that she let them steal, and the page in her book headed *Thefts* soon filled up with her pointed black script. Our father is a different matter, however, and our increasing success in keeping him off the highways has meant there's less saved than in previous years.

At last James and I emerge into the clearing. It is an overwhelming relief to see the tower still safe, a haven. "You'd better blow the horn, James," I gasp as we make a dash across the open ground. He holds on to the hawthorn tree by the gatehouse, bent double, getting his breath back. I open the door and grab the battered ram's-horn from its niche in the wall. James seizes it from me, and blows.

The sound freezes in the air. It is like doom. Gooseflesh rises on my arms and legs. James keeps blowing, getting into his rhythm now, twice outside the main door towards the valley, then up the spiral stairway, once at each slit window. The effect is immediate. Kate's screams echo up from the cellars. Thudding feet start running on the upper floors. Leo's voice shouts in the valley, and the cows, under the thwack of his hazel tine, start bellowing. Whatever is the watchman doing? He must be asleep, not to have seen the warning smoke on the hill and over the water.

He was. As James and I emerge on to the battlements he is rubbing his eyes and staggering about, his hair ruffled, and a smell of ale rising from him that could have ignited the beacon unaided. For a moment I feel mad with fury.

"Henry!" I slap him hard across the face with the back of my hand, the one which wears Grandmother's turquoise ring. It leaves a broad weal and breaks his skin. Tiny wells of blood rise along the mark. It also wakes him up.

"Mis... Mistress Beatrice," he splutters. "You'd no call to do that."

"The Scots are coming, you great boggart!" I hit him again for good measure with the tar torch, before I go to light it at the living-hall fire, one floor down. I can hear the combined braying of James's horn and Kate's screaming as I run down the steps and up again, carrying the roaring torch. By then my father, Verity, Kate and two henchmen, William and Martinus, have arrived on the battlements, and have begun stacking stones and arrows by the parapet. Kate's screaming has dropped to a whimper now. She is terrified of the Scots, and of many things. Her nerves have never been the same since the day years ago when this tiny woman, with her wonderful singing voice, wild grey hair like a dandelion seed-head and a serious limp caused by stampeding cattle during a childhood Scottish raid, was accused of witchcraft. It was because she told fortunes, inaccurately it has to be said. She was also frequently accompanied by a black cat, mother of my cat Caesar. It was enough, for those looking for someone to blame for their own misfortunes. It was the old parson who accused her, from the pulpit one Sunday. Before the matter could get out of hand, as these things so often do, Mother stood up and faced him in the nave of the church and outquoted him text by text from the Bible, suggesting that he who was without sin should cast the first stone. Or better still, eat it and choke for shame. I was astonished at my mother's knowing, scornful voice, and at the sniggers that ran among the rows of people standing tense and motionless in the packed church. I didn't understand what it all meant then, but heard tales later, when I was older, of this priest having a bastard in every village.

The old parson, perhaps realising that if he had Kate hanged he would have no one to sing so beautifully at his weddings and funerals, not to mention the annual two-village barn dance at which the sight of him performing a Cumberland square reel with his cassock tucked into his hose was not unknown, marched out of church that day, and afterwards said no more of the matter.

Witches hang and heretics burn, but there are fewer hangings and burnings under this queen than under the last one. Old people still speak fearfully of Queen Mary's days. Bloody Mary, they call her. With the change of queen from Mary to Elizabeth the tide has turned from burning Protestants to burning Catholics. Burning those who disagree with you is a hard habit to shake off. We heard news recently of the burnings of some Catholics just a few hours' ride south of us in Lancaster, but up here no one cares much what faith you follow so long as you are discreet. Witchcraft, of course, is another matter.

Now the old priest is dead, replaced by a younger man who declares that witchcraft does not exist, heresy scarcely matters and that we had all better damn well love each other or he'll know the reason why. He took over Verity's and my lessons from the old parson. Sadly, these have stopped now that I am sixteen.

I light my second beacon of the day. The tar barrels ignite at once with a huff of sound, and snarl like animals as they burn. I step down hurriedly as the heat hits me. Verity is handing out swords, bows and clubs, as more henchmen and Germaine appear at the top of the stairway. A grim air of calm hangs over us.

Germaine refuses the bow which Verity offers her, and goes to fetch her own. Germaine is our only other female servant besides Kate. She is tall and dark and very beautiful, and plays a variety of musical instruments with a variety of lack of talent. She is supposed to teach music and needlework to Verity and myself, and do the mending. Instead she spends most of her time entertaining Father.

I go downstairs with William and Henry to watch them lug our heavy old hagbut out of its cupboard on the east stairs and across the passage into the men's common room. At Barrowbeck we cannot afford many firearms in the way that some of the bigger fortresses can. Our hagbut is inaccurate, slow to load and terrifyingly loud. Its eccentric angle of fire is such that it is more effective aimed from the common room, half way down the tower. When he was a young man, my father used to carry it into battle on his shoulder.

The men latch the weapon on to its stand and tip it awkwardly backwards, like a cannon, for me to load. I uncap a horn of gunpowder and ram shot and gunpowder down the barrel, wadding it into place. "Better oil the hinges," I suggest, extracting the ramrod and propping it by the wall for next time. I filter some fine gunpowder into the priming pan. "I'll get you some lard from the kitchen. You need it to swing up more easily than that for reloading." The acrid smell of gunpowder is in my nose and on my hands as I hurry downstairs.

Now I am beginning to worry about Mother. Where is she? Is she still safely with Aunt Juniper, or is she in the woods on her way home? If the latter, then surely she will have heard the horn and seen the beacon, and will either hurry home or find somewhere to hide. Back on the battlements I work my way through the crowd to where Germaine is flexing her longbow. Most of us just have ordinary bows, but Germaine insists on using this six-foot monstrosity with its silk and flaxen string. I have to say, though, that she does tend to hit things with it.

"Germaine?" I take care to be polite. "Would you please take charge of closing all the shutters, and later when we're all in, wind down the grille on the door and open the wolf-pit? Can I just leave all those things to you? Oh, and please don't forget to *call* 'Wolf-pit open'. We don't want a repeat of what happened to poor old Edmund."

She carries on flexing her bow, and replies, "You have an excessive amount of responsibility for one so young, Beatrice, and it has had a most unfortunate effect on you."

I turn away in irritation. Henry, who has re-emerged on to the battlements, overhears, and suppresses a grin. His face is still bleeding in a row of gleaming droplets. I am regretting my outburst of temper. I should like to apologise, but the words won't quite come.

"Henry." I approach him. He looks minded to ignore me, but I stand in front of him. "Come with me, Henry. Let's go and help Leo round up the cattle and bring the pigs up the hill." I look round the full sweep of horizon. Smoke now rises from the Pike, and distantly from the direction of my cousins' pele tower at Mere Point, as well as behind us on Beacon Hill, but of the raiders there is no sign.

Chapter 4

It is very quiet in the woods. The birds are silent and the squirrels and deer are nowhere to be seen. It is as if everyone and everything were waiting for the marauders to arrive. Yet by now, mid-afternoon of the following day, it seems almost certain that the beacon fire across the bay was a false alarm, a bush fire perhaps. It would not be the first time.

In previous raids we have scarcely had time to get our cattle into the tower, let alone the sheep up into the woods. Surrounding homesteaders have not stood a chance, and their houses have been ripped bare of everything, then burned to the ground. Many of them have lost their lives defending their homes. At Barrowbeck Tower we are in a stronger position. Our thick walls protect us and we are excellent shots. We do not fight hand-to-hand, but shoot down arrows on the invaders, gavlockes with forked metal heads, or shafts with flaming tar-soaked rags bound to their tips.

This time it has been possible to gather all the homesteaders, with their cattle, ponies, pigs and goats, into the lower rooms. The crush is terrible. The smell is worse. The silence of these woods is a relief after the dreadful racket of the animals. All I can hear now are my own footsteps, and the tinkle of the belwether as sheep wander in dense woodland.

Our beacon is dying down, though it still throws out a ferocious heat in the afternoon sun. I am on my way to damp down and make safe the fire on Beacon Hill. I also have some slight hope of meeting Mother. Mother looks after our dairy, and by now will be fretting about curds left to stand too long, and cream on the turn before it can be churned into butter, despite the coolness of its rock cave.

I am too hot in my grey woollen gown. My byggen cap is sticking to my forehead. I rest for a moment, and from habit gather a few dry sticks to replenish the kindling on Beacon Hill. I have taken the less known path because it seems safer. Off to my left is an old hermit's cottage in the hazel thicket. It is half overgrown with brambles since the hermit died of a quinsy last winter. I tell myself I could hide there, if the Scots came now.

This way up Beacon Hill is hard going, overgrown through little use. When I reach the top the smoky air makes me cough. I rest a moment, then pile stones round the collapsed ashes of the fire, and shovel damp soil into the middle. We will prepare it ready for next time once the embers have cooled. A false twilight has spread across the valley and the bay, from the smoking fires, but the wind will soon clear it. On my way back down through the woods I feel a surge of cheerfulness. A distant brush-fire has taken a day from our lives, but no matter. Tonight all the beacons will die down, and tomorrow Mother will come home.

As I emerge from the trees I do not notice, at first, the thin, dark line streaming down the far side of the valley. I am out into the open before I see them, careering between the windblown trees on the Pike, racing down the distant, pebble-strewn screes.

It had seemed an impossible slope, almost vertical. They have never come that way before. I realise, all in a flash, that they must have been hiding up there on the Pike, waiting for us to relax, knowing they would not be expected from that direction because we thought the sheer screes protected us. How long have they been watching? Days, perhaps. The speed the steepness gives them is terrifying.

I am out in the open, but they have not seen me yet. I start to run towards the tower. The Scots are spreading out in an arc. Now I can hear them shouting. I can see their saffron coats, goatskin jerkins and brown and green draperies flapping about their knees. They have bows over their shoulders; a few, horrifyingly, have crossbows. At their waists are axes, dorks and cutlasses. Some carry muskets, and others, most ominously of all, scaling ladders. They are coming faster than I am. It is like running into the gates of Hell. For a moment I consider hiding in the woods, but it is too late. The outer edges of their line are spreading into a circle that will join arms behind me. There is no way back. Suddenly they see me. A great shout goes up. Individual Scots break free of the line and run straight at me. The ground is shaking under their feet as I reach the tower door. Their hands stretch out for me. Their sweat suffocates me.

I had been afraid that no one would hear me or let me in, but the grille goes up fast, the door opens and Verity and Martinus pull me into the gatehouse. I stagger back against the wall, but something is wrong. The door will not shut behind me. Verity and Martinus throw their weight at it but the Scots are pushing from the other side, and slowly the door is opening again. I try to wind down the grille, but it will not move. I give up, realising they have jammed it, and instead add my strength to those trying to push the door shut. Laughter from outside mocks us. A cutlass pokes through the widening gap.

"They're making it easy for us this time, laddies," calls a voice next to the hinge, a hand's breadth from my ear.

"Father! Send down more men!" Verity shouts through the inner door. Footsteps come running from above, but they are going to be too late. The door is opening now and there is nothing we can do to stop it. Those coming down the stairs behind us ought to bar the inner door against us, and safeguard the rest of the tower, but I know they will not. None of us here dares let go to seize weapons. Martinus gestures desperately to Verity and me to get behind the inner door and barricade ourselves in. Verity mutters, "And give you the pleasure of finishing off the bastards on your own?" except she does not describe them so genteelly.

The hairy hand and arm holding the cutlass pushes further through the gap. There is an explosion – our hagbut. Gunshots thud against the walls. In a brief, quiet moment I hear the hiss and whistle of arrows. Now James is here. He does not add his weight to pushing at the door, but instead seizes the horn from its niche and brings it up hard against the elbow that is pushing through the gap. The hand springs convulsively open and the cutlass clatters down, but the arm does not withdraw. Instead, with a jolt from outside, the door opens faster. Then a hand comes from behind me, a hand holding a sword. With a swift up and downward chop, it slashes at the arm. It is Kate. If her angle had been better she might have severed the limb. An inhuman scream spirals out of audible pitch. Blood spurts, and the arm is pulled back. I know I shall never again watch with equanimity while Kate carves the meat.

We all hurl ourselves at the door then, and at last it slams shut. Father is here now, and he crashes the six bolts and three heavy iron bars into their slots, fumbling with

41

drunken haste. I steady his hand as he feeds metal into metal. Martinus drags at the handle which lowers the iron grille outside, and as he puts his full weight behind it there is a cracking noise, and it finally turns. Somebody outside yells as the descending grille hits them. James picks up the horn and restores it to its place.

The battle is long and terrible. It is the worst I remember. Father stands at the window of the living hall with his antiquated longbow, pumping arrows into the enemy. We don't bother with crossbows here at Barrowbeck. At this height and range they have no particular virtue, and are too slow to reload, though the Scots put them to terrifying use from below. The extra power sends their arrows high over our battlements where our henchmen crouch, firing back. Behind them some of the young men and women from the valley kneel in the shelter of the beacon turret, binding arrow points in linen, dipping them in hot tar and setting them alight before passing them forward for firing. We all have short swords and knives at our belts, in case hand-to-hand combat should become necessary. Verity and James operate the catapult. James hefts the stones and Verity pulls back the lever. Occasionally James just throws a particularly heavy stone over the battlements. Downstairs Leo stands watch on the outer door, ready to bar the inner door if needs be. In the kitchen Kate boils lard for pouring on the enemy, and Germaine carries it up the stairs in wooden pails, cursing under her breath as homesteaders get in her way and the stairs grow greasy underfoot.

Many of the valley homesteaders who herded their animals into the tower are now huddled in the lower rooms with them. There are so many this time that in places it is difficult to move. We have put James's black cattle in the kitchen with Kate. All the animals are going mad with terror. Their lowing and whinnying and squealing fill our ears, and the stink of them rises up the stairs in great waves.

My job is to go round checking that all possible entry points are defended. I have not forgotten the rope scaling ladders which I saw earlier. As I reach the gatehouse on one of my patrols, I find Leo looking very grim.

"They're trying to fire the door, lady."

I look down, and see a curl of smoke feathering out of a narrow crack at the base of the door.

"It will never burn, Leo. Thank the Lord we treated it in time."

"Mebbe best get Mistress Kate to soak some leather for under it."

"I'll do that." I move towards the kitchen, then stop. "Did you hear that?"

We both listen. Leo's mouth tightens. "Grappling irons. They're trying to get up the walls."

"They must have hooked into one of the windows. Quick, Leo. If you start looking I'll get some of the others to go round too." As I speak, a homesteader

43

comes rushing down from the battlements to tell us the Scots are scaling the walls. There is a flurry of commotion from above. Leo and I quickly bar the inner door and I hurry through the arch to the kitchen. Here people from the valley are tearing up linen for arrows and bandages, feeding and tending their animals, soothing their babies. At the far end of the kitchen James's black cows are imprisoned by the long table, knee deep in straw and dung, lowing and stamping and rolling their eyes. Over the fire another cauldron of fat is heating, suspended from the greasy, dripping rackencrock. Shiny white gobs of lard slide from the sides of the cauldron, sink in the melted oil, then surface again, smaller. I ask some of the homesteaders to soak strips of leather for under the door, and others to spread out through the tower and check the windows for grappling irons. In the end, though, I am the one who finds the first ugly metal hook.

I go into the men's common room and find Henry dead on the floor, our hagbut toppled from its stand, gunpowder drizzling out of its barrel. Henry has a great wound to his head where the grappling iron hit him, before it lodged tightly under the stone sill of the window. Now it rattles and shakes as someone climbs the rope ladder beneath.

There is no time. A face appears at the window. It all happens too fast. The bright hazel eyes are wide and wild, the beardless mouth young and reckless. He would have hauled himself in, but in the shock of seeing me, his defences are down, and he is too slow.

I take his face in my hands and push. With an arching cry he somersaults away backwards, out of sight.

I send his hook spinning after him, but I cannot watch him, or it, hit the ground. Instead, I race from room to room searching for more hooks. Between us the homesteaders and I find three more. We dislodge them with pokers and shovels, sending them and their human burdens hurtling to earth.

Whether it is the hurling down of these foolhardy climbers that finally makes the Scots lose heart, I do not know, but by the time I reach the battlements again, they are in retreat. Father's henchmen send a score of flaming arrows after them for good measure, but the fleeing Scots are quickly out of range, heading down the valley towards the sea, carrying their wounded, and leaving behind them twelve or fifteen ghastly, staring corpses on the bloody, ashen, pig-greasy turf.

Chapter 5

None of us emerges until the following day. Double watch is kept all night. By next morning the whole area smells like a slaughterhouse, and a thick crust of black flies has formed on the outside of the tower. They creep in through the window slits and buzz in our faces, grotesquely unable to differentiate between the living and the dead. Outside, they swarm on the bodies. On the grass they move in patterns, forming and re-forming like fishermen's nets on the sea.

My father, sober and out of bed for once, leads prayers of thanksgiving for our deliverance, as we all stand crushed together in the men's common room. On our side only Henry is dead, though several more of the henchmen are wounded. Henry lies now in our tiny chapel over the gatehouse. Father prays for his soul. He even, in what seems to me like a fit of remarkable generosity, offers up a brief prayer for the souls of the fallen Scots.

"He'd best not let the parson hear him praying for folks' souls," Germaine whispers to me. "That's Popish stuff."

I look at her. Is she loyal to no one, not even my father? Not that there seems much point in his prayers. I cannot believe that God listens to my father. He might as well pray to the elder tree in the thicket, the way some people round here still do.

"Amen," chorus the homesteaders. I look across their bowed heads. In a few minutes they will have to walk out past those bloating corpses and down the valley to see which of their stick and mud homes are still standing. Their children, tired from two nights on the common rooms' floors, are mardy and whimpering. The stench from the livestock is overwhelming even up here now, and it blends with the smell of carnage below to create a foul miasma which clogs our noses. Several times I pass people being sick out of windows.

Later, most of us go down to help redistribute the livestock. Buckets of milk stand all along the downstairs passageways. The floors of the lower rooms are thick with dung. Most of the cattle are in distress because the crowded conditions have not made for adequate milking. They skip and kick as they are released down the curving slope to the cellars, then shoulder each other along the underground passage, through the stone arch under the dairy, up the slope at the other end where part of the flagstone floor has been removed, and out into the barmkin, pursued by Leo shouting, "Git on, yer great lummocks."

Two pigs, herded by their owner out of the barmkin, rush towards where the bodies lie. Children watch in fascination to see if the pigs are to be allowed to eat the bodies, and Kate mutters, "Reet pigs an' all," and ushers the children away, while the swineherd hurries his charges up the hill.

Father yells, "Bury the dead!" I see that his hands are shaking from lack of drink. I put my arm round him and embrace him, then join the homesteaders and help them sort out their animals.

Later I go up to the chapel to see Henry's body. Bright sunlight pours in through the high window and shimmers on the embroidered altar cloth and the linen sheet covering him. Four candles burn, two at his head and two at his feet. The four spiked silver candle prickets represent Matthew, Mark, Luke and John. The old priest said they were Popish folly, but the new priest says they are beautiful. I lift one of the candles, spilling hot wax on my hand, and hold it close to see Henry better. I can feel my burnt skin puckering under the cooling wax. Henry's cheeks are smooth and white, his chin dark with stubble. The wound from the grappling iron stands out in shades of black and purple, and below it, the graze from my ring is raised and red. I touch it with the hand I used to slap him, then turn away and bring my hand down on the spike. I am not brave. It is a gash, no more. The blood runs over my fingers, through the turquoise ring, and I walk unsteadily back downstairs.

Mother has arrived home, and with her are Hugh and Gerald. Verity and I stand outside the tower amongst the piled dungheaps which Kate and Leo are still shovelling out, and hold her tightly and cry.

"Are you all right?" she demands. "I was dreadfully worried about you."

"Yes. Are *you* all right, Mother?" I see that her cheeks are very red and healthy-looking, and despite her stated anxiety she has the appearance of someone rather pleased with herself. Hugh and Gerald grin at us, and take themselves off upstairs to have a tankard of ale in the common room with the men. All of them are now back from burying the bodies of the Scots in a clearing on the hill behind Barrow Wood. Henry's body will travel the Old Corpse Road to Wraithwaite tomorrow, for burial in the churchyard. Now the men have been given a quart of ale each to help them forget the dreadful sights they have seen and the dreadful textures they have touched.

Mother, Verity and I go up to Verity's room and sit on the cushioned stone benches along the walls, leaning back against the pictorial tapestries which Verity weaves. We are all very tired. Kate, unasked, brings hot, mulled wine.

"Did they attack Mere Point?" I ask. Mother shakes her head.

"No, but we'd just let the cattle out again, and they took those. They're getting too darned clever by half, hiding and waiting like that. I was frantic when I heard they were attacking Barrowbeck. A lad said they'd got into the tower, but Aunt Juniper wouldn't let me come back until now. Even then she insisted on sending Hugh and Gerald with me. Not that they needed much persuading." She says this with more hope than conviction.

We talk until Kate rings the bell for supper, then we go up to eat in the living hall. Lately Germaine has been eating here with us, instead of in the kitchen with Kate and the henchmen. As usual, our food is half cold by the time Kate has slogged up the east stairs with it. She bangs down the pewter dishes in front of us. I believe she thinks we should pay for our privileges.

"Wouldn't you prefer to eat in the kitchen, Germaine?" Verity asks gently. When she speaks gently, we all know to watch out. "You'd get your food hot from the hearth then. In fact, I think I might start eating in the kitchen myself."

"A good idea, mistress. Perhaps we all should." Germaine helps herself to more of the congealing mutton in its puddle of yellow grease.

Father throws Verity a look and says, "That's quite enough of that, Daughter."

For much of the rest of the meal, talk is of the tower's defences. It annoys me that Father booms on to Hugh and Gerald about improving the defences of the two towers, when he does so little about it in practice. Hugh takes my hand under the table and gives it a squeeze. I stare at him, quite startled. He asks my father, "Are you riding tonight, Uncle?" A shocked silence falls. It is an unspoken rule that we never discuss my father's regrettable tendency to rob travellers on the queen's highway.

My father smiles at his nephew. "Likely as not. You wish to come?"

Hugh smiles respectfully back. "Nay. Thanks Uncle. I'm as tall as I care to be."

After the meal, Verity and our two cousins and I walk up towards Barrow Wood in the dampness of early evening. Hugh says, "It was time someone said something. You are all too careful of him. Being squire of Barrowbeck won't save him from having his neck stretched, if they catch him."

"Oh..." I sigh. "I know, but you don't have to live with him. You had a more kindly response from him than any of us would have."

It is exhilarating to be free of the constrictions and smell of the tower. Hugh takes my hand again, and I see Verity's eyes widen.

"Well, Cousin." Hugh speaks quietly to me, excluding the others. "How are you truly, after your ordeal?"

"Well enough, thank you Cousin." I feel far too unnerved to make any pretence of proper conversation. I see, mildly alarmed, that we have now lost sight of the other two amongst the trees. I decide that frankness is my best defence. I lift our clasped hands.

"What am I supposed to make of this, Hugh?"

He flushes. Hugh is very fair-skinned, with pale, straight hair, fairer than his brother. I know that he is considered handsome, and I can see that one could think him so, but to me he is still so much my childhood companion that his comeliness or otherwise is irrelevant. We face each other in the darkening forest. "How do you feel about our families' plans for us?" he asks me.

"Hugh... I'm not ready to consider them yet..." I clear my throat and try again. "Of course, I love you as a cousin..." I feel desperately disturbed by his closeness. Never, even in our most frightening games as children, has Hugh seemed threatening, but he seems threatening now. "It's too soon," I falter. "I hadn't thought it would come so soon."

"Your father and mine have indicated their wishes, Beatie, but it doesn't have to be soon." He lets go of my hand. "I should have liked it to be soon... it's not just our fathers' wish... but you're two years younger. I can wait. Could we... perhaps... try to see each other differently? I have to confess that your friendly, jesting attitude towards me makes you rather unapproachable on these matters."

There is a pause. The light is fading. Hugh seems like a stranger. We walk in the direction of the old hermit's cottage, no longer holding hands, no longer speaking. Green light filters through the leaves, down to the forest floor. When we reach a corner of the crumbling boundary wall we sit down on it, side by side in the moss-coloured dimness. I turn to Hugh. "We know each other too well, Hugh. I cannot think of you in the way you wish."

He puts his arm round my shoulders briefly, then releases me. "I won't ask you again until the winter, Cousin." After a moment he adds, "I would do anything for you, Beatrice. I would walk through the quicksands across the bay for you."

I stand up. "Now you're getting carried away, Hugh." I feel uneasy and uncomfortable, and I think at first that Hugh's words are the cause. Then I realise that there was a noise. I turn slowly. Surely the hermit's cottage is still uninhabited? The noise is repeated, a crackling, shifting sound.

"Hugh, I heard something. Did you hear it?"

He stands up and looks around. "What did you hear?"

"I don't know. A twig. A movement."

The awareness of someone, a presence, is suddenly very powerful. It was the feeling I had on the Pike, and on Beacon Hill, but now a hundred, a thousand times stronger.

"The old man's dead, isn't he?" Hugh asks.

"Yes. Perhaps someone else has taken over the cottage," I suggest, before we can start talking about ghosts and goblins. Hugh begins to creep round the low wattle hut. A branch snaps under his foot. I lift my skirts and step over the broken wall, then move cautiously along the front of the dwelling. A narrow window slot gives on to a dark interior, from which a foul, ancient odour seeps. The hermit was not known for his cleanliness. I move to the door and push it open and peer in. From what I can

53

see of them, the matted rushes on the floor look as if they have been there since Queen Mary's day. It is impossible to see anything else.

Suddenly, a buffeting wind shakes the woods. The patchy cloud cover overhead shifts, and tightly woven tree branches rattle apart. A bright hem of light swirls through the forest, and briefly illuminates the inside of the cottage. I can see more clearly the rushes on the floor, rank and mouldy, a battered iron skillet lying upended, a heap of droppings left by the hermit's goat. There is something else too, a bundle of brown and green cloth lying in a corner where broken reeds hang down from the roof. The bundle moves. It is a man. I can see his face, bruised and swollen. It is a face I recognise.

Chapter 6

*H*ugh looks pleased when I take his hand and lead him back through the woods to the point where the paths diverge. My throat is dry and my head pounding. It amounts to treason, to conceal the presence of a Scot, and the penalty is to be burnt at the stake. The virtual certainty that it is the young man whose face I pushed from the tower window is the only excuse I can give myself. I can still feel his soft skin where my fingers pressed, and the horrific ease of pushing him away into unsupporting air.

"I'll walk with you back to the tower," Hugh says, but I tell him I want to be alone for a while, and I watch his vanishing back as he takes the path towards Mere Point. When I reach the meadow in front of the tower, I can see that Verity is already home, standing on the battlements watching the sun go down beyond the bay. Owls are hooting close by, and in the far distance a faint howl comes from the woods across the water. I know it is only foxes, though in a bad winter the wolves of the Scottish borders have been known to round the bay as far as Milnthorpe.

I sit on a tree stump and think about the extraordinary course of action which I have taken. The Scot is obviously injured, possibly badly injured, otherwise he would have fled with his fellow raiders. He must have crawled away from the battle scene after I pushed him from the window, and been unable to rejoin his comrades in time when they fled. He is my enemy, but it is my fault he is injured. On the other hand, he attacked us first. I should have told Hugh, and now it is my duty to tell my father, who will send at once to Milnthorpe for a magistrate, and the Scot will be hanged. Instead, I am going home to collect food and water for him.

I stand up and walk quickly towards the tower. The sheep stop their soft chomping as I hurry by, and scatter as if my urgency threatened them. I let myself in quietly. The kitchen is empty, the fire sunk low in the hearth. I move round as silently as I can, collecting bread, cheese and milk. I put them in a basket, then creep down to the root cellar and stand a leather bottle under the spigot of the copper water cistern to fill. While I wait, I look round the shifting, candlelit gloom. No animals were allowed in the root cellar, but the passage to it became heavily soiled with their waste, and even in here it still stinks. The remains of the winter carrots and turnips seem contaminated.

When the flagon is full I hammer in a wooden bung with my fist, and creep back up the passage to the kitchen. It is still empty. Outside, shadows have stretched across the clearing in my absence. Over the bay a line of purple light still shows, but around me it is almost dark. I walk towards the trees, the basket and flagon concealed under my cloak.

Among the trees it is very dark indeed. I stumble several times over tree roots, even though I know the path so well. I dare not look behind me, nor to the sides. The stillness of twilight is gone, and there are sounds in the undergrowth. When I branch off from the main path I can scarcely see at all. I try to force my mind to more mundane matters than wolves and witches.

Suddenly I have reached the boundary of the hovel. I almost fall over it in the dark. In places the wall is completely covered with brambles. They fill the clearing and even climb up the wattle and daub of the cottage walls. Stones have fallen from the boundary wall into the gateway, and I have to pick my way carefully over them. One stone rocks beneath my feet and almost pitches me head-first into the thorns. It also, with its clatter, announces my arrival.

What if I was mistaken and he is not injured? What if, even at this moment, he is waiting behind a tree? I put down the basket and flagon by the worm-eaten doorway, and flee.

Only two candles are burning in the kitchen. Verity has coaxed the fire back to life and is sitting with her feet up on Kate's oak settle, watching the pot over the fire start to steam. She points to the bark box where she keeps dried camomile flowers.

"Do you want a bedtime drink?" Her voice sounds normal, but I can see that something is wrong. She has changed into her cream linen nightsmock and grey woollen nightgown, and her hair is down round her shoulders. She would look angelic if her face were not puffy and red, with a large spot on one cheek and shiny swellings beneath her eyes. Verity has been crying.

"Thank you. I could do with something soothing."

She raises her eyebrows. She had not been going to ask, but if I was going to tell, well then, that was different. The pot boils, and she ladles hot water on to the wizened camomile flowers in our pewter mugs. The flowers sink and float, sink and float, briefly regaining their white and yellow fullness. My lips brush the petals as I take a sip.

"Is it Hugh?" she asks.

"Yes, I think Father and Uncle have been getting at him. I suppose it's inevitable."

Verity slops her drink down her nightgown. "Inevitable? Nothing's inevitable, Beatie. I think you've taken leave of your senses, heading into the forest hand in hand with Hugh. I could scarcely believe my eyes. Hugh and Gerald are two more like Father. You'll be nothing if you give in to one of them."

I stare at her. "But surely we have no choice? What will happen to the farms if we don't keep them in the family?"

"No different from what happens to them now, I daresay. We don't have to sell ourselves to keep our land."

" I know that. But..." I feel I must do our cousins justice. "... Hugh and Gerald aren't like Father, Verity. They're our friends."

"Just wait till they're husbands, and then you'll see. You'll go to Hugh at Mere Point, and leave your home and everything you love. Gerald, who is not my friend, by the way, and whom I dislike rather a lot, will come here and want to take over. No, I will not have it. You and I can look after Barrowbeck ourselves." She extracts a camomile flower from her teeth and flicks it into the hearth.

"You mean not marry at all? They wouldn't allow it. I wouldn't put it past Father to disinherit us."

Verity moves her feet to make room for me at the other end of the settle. "Aye, and I wouldn't put it past thee and me, Sister, to pay a visit to Magistrate Chantry at Milnthorpe some cloudless night when a passing lordship is being held up on the highway."

I look at her sceptically. She smiles. "All right, maybe you're right, but I'd have a mighty urge to threaten him with it." She reaches for the poker and turns a log so that its red underside throws out heat into the room. Firelight falls across her face as she leans back and looks at me. "It will not happen, Beatie. They will not force us to marry. Not that you'd need forcing if Parson Becker were to stand the wrong side of the altar with you."

My own face burns. "Verity, your brain is fevered," I snap. "Anyway, Parson Becker is already wedded – to his work."

"Hm..." Her eyes narrow in a faint grin, and I am so glad to see the tears gone that I forgive her look of triumph. It is rather a thrilling thought, anyway. The fire crumbles into pink-tinged ash, and just one single, cold flame flickers at its centre. I kiss the top of my sister's head and retire to bed, to remember the feeling of Parson Becker's rough black clothes under my hands, the day he comforted me after I fell off my pony. The Scot, and what I did to help him, seem unimportant now, distant and unreal. I push them from my mind. He is likely long gone already.

Chapter 7

In the morning I am not so sure. I know I am going to have to go back and find out.

I hurry through the morning's tasks and am about to set off straight after our midday meal when word arrives that the queen's purvey man is on his way from Lancaster to collect our taxes. Father insists I go down to help Leo move the cattle around. We put out our thinnest, scraggiest ones to pick away pathetically at thistles in the fields, and drive the good strong beasts through the barmkin and into the underground chambers. Verity is sent round to tell everyone to put on their poorest clothes. Unfortunately for the purvey man, news of his coming travels even more efficiently than news of the Scots.

Mother, who dislikes this deception that we are so poor as to be well nigh untaxable, always gives him one of her ripe cheeses from the dairy. Dense and dark-rinded, they are strong enough to cure the ague. The purvey man says he takes it as a present for the queen, and perhaps he does, but we think he probably keeps it for himself. In return, he brings us ready-made soap from a place called Bankside in London. It is paler and less greasy than our own home-made soap, and a great luxury.

It turns out, when the purvey man arrives, that he has been robbed on the highway, at Kerne Forth, the night before. Father expresses shock and horror. The rest of us avoid each other's eyes. Father offers to give the man a little extra contribution for himself, to help him on his way, after such a distressing event. When I go down to the root cellar to fill a flagon with water for the Scot, I find Father there, sorting through coins so that he doesn't give the man his own money back.

I should try to stop Father's secret life of crime, I know that, but I fear his temper, and anyway, it would be pointless. He is in thrall to highway robbery as he is in thrall to drink, and I dread that one day he will be caught. I suppose a proper sense of right and wrong would make me want him caught, so that innocent people are no longer terrorised and their belongings stolen. I must therefore assume that I do not possess a proper sense of right and wrong. I knew that anyway, otherwise I should not be protecting a Scot.

As I finally set off for the hermit's cottage, I meet James at the edge of the clearing. Anxiety rises in my throat. Am I never to be able to get away? James has come up the back way from his farm with eggs and honey for us. At the tower we do not keep chickens and bees ourselves but are paid in eggs and fowl and honey and beeswax by James and the homesteaders, for our protection. James looks at my flagon and oilskin package and tells me he will leave his basket at the tower and then walk with me. I assure him I'll be delighted to have his company, for I am off to have a quiet afternoon of prayer and contemplation in the chapel on the cliffs. James remembers an urgent appointment elsewhere.

It is damp and cool today. The path squelches under my feet. Further along, where the ground rises and becomes stony, I meet my little horse, Saint Hilda, clopping down towards the meadow, and I give her a small, brown-spotted apple which I had intended to eat myself. It is the last one salvaged from the straw in the corner of the root cellar, and very precious, since there will be no more until autumn. Saint Hilda snuffles her white velvet breath into my palm, and crunches the fruit sloppily between her big, yellow teeth. I have a nasty feeling that after my lie to James I deserve something horrible to happen to me in the woods, perhaps to see the Green Man himself or some other malevolent woodland spirit who will punish me for pretending to be on a holy errand when I am on a most unholy one. The apple is a small penance, but perhaps it will do.

I reach the beck. Fast-moving water glitters through

ground mist. The woods are quiet, apart from the sound of water. I duck beneath low hanging branches and move through dense woodland where drifts of wood anemones make white patterns on the forest floor. From this direction, the cottage is invisible until I am almost on it. Trees and brambles enclose it tightly from behind. All around me wet leaves drip water down thin stems. I think of the Green Man with his leafy fingers and knothole eyes, and of chained spirits in trees, so jealous of our freedom that we must touch wood to acknowledge and appease them, if we should happen to feel too pleased with ourselves.

I creep round the cottage to the front. Nothing stirs. The cottage is silent inside and out. I shiver. Perhaps the Scot is now dead. It might be better for him if he were. I bunch up my skirts and edge through a gap in the surrounding wall. I keep out of range of the door and push through the brambles to one of the window slots. The remains of a transparent oiled linen rag hang here, where it once served as windowpane. The cottage is dark inside. I cannot see anything. I drag my skirts free of the brambles and move to the doorway. The basket and flagon have gone from the threshold but the door still stands half open, as it did before. I step inside.

The sight and smell hit me at the same time. The Scot is there, indeed, but not as I have ever seen any human being. He lies on his side, twisted out of shape with agony. His eyes are rolled back in his head; his mouth is open and frothing. Spittle and filth cover his face. His arm is clearly broken. No natural elbow ever bent at that angle. A grey glister of fever covers every part of his skin that is visible. His jaws jerk in a grotesque, spasmic champing motion.

He is lying on a blackened straw pallet. I step over to him, appalled. I should never have left him to get into this state. His legs, beneath the filthy brown and green blanket girdled about him, kick convulsively. His rolling eyes circle past me. He cannot see me. I crouch next to him and whisper, "It's all right." I can feel the heat off him before I even touch him. I put my hand to his forehead. It is burning under a layer of greasy sweat. "There now." I push the hair off his face. "We need some water." I look round the room. The flagon stands in a corner. It is still half full. I hold it to the Scotsman's lips. They move weakly and liquid dribbles down his chin. I support his head and drip water into his mouth.

"That's good. Take some more." I ease a few more drops past his clenched teeth. The stink of him is frightful, and my stomach heaves. Kate always says you can tell an illness by the smell of it. I wonder what she would make of this.

By the time I have forced the equivalent of half a cup of water past his lips, the Scotsman's legs have ceased their convulsions and his eyes have closed. He lies back heavily against my supporting arm.

"I must clean you," I whisper. I stand up and realise

65

that I must clean this place, too, if he is to recover. The cottage consists of just one small room. The only furniture is the straw pallet. The rushes on the floor are black and evil-smelling, and dotted with droppings from the hermit's goat. Brown beetles scuttle amongst the mouldering stalks, their dry legs clacking. Tiny, reddish-brown fleas dance round my ankles. I decide to clean the Scotsman first, then the cottage.

In the valley we cover our floors in winter with fresh rushes from Mistholme Moss, the swamp over towards the next village, and in summer with sweet herbs and dried grass. I will strew the floor with wormwood to get rid of the fleas, bay to get rid of the beetles, rosemary, lavender and sweet woodruff to make the air wholesome.

I use water from the flagons, then more from the beck, to bathe the Scotsman. I have only the cloths that wrapped the bread inside the oilskin, but they must suffice. First I clean his face, coaxing dirt and grimy fragments away, then his neck and shoulders and legs. It seems strange to be bathing a grown man, and I am glad that his senses have abandoned him. When I come to look at his injured arm, I try to ease his sleeve back gently, but still a howl of anguish escapes him. I wait, but there is no sign of returning consciousness, so I persevere. His upper arm is a horrid sight. Raw flesh is suppurating on the bone, and as I peer more closely, I can see the bone itself. I realise that this arm may not be saved. I have seen wounds like this before, where the limb has had to be removed by our local sawbones, a fearsome giant who lives on the cliffs, and whom we call the Cockleshell Man. Occasionally the doctor will come from Milnthorpe to try to save a limb, but his fees are high, and most people in the valley cannot afford him.

"You need a doctor, my poor enemy," I tell the Scot, "but if I send for the physician he will hand you to the authorities and you will hang."

"Aye."

I nearly collapse.

"Get on wi' it, lass. Clean me up. Let me die washed, at least."

I pull myself together and reply coldly, "You'll not die, Scotsman."

"Well it'll not be for the want of you trying. Why would ye want to save me now?"

"Did you expect me to help you over the windowsill and into the tower? I was protecting myself and my family. That doesn't mean to say I'll leave a defenceless man to rot to death now." I take my knife from my belt and cut his sleeve from his arm. His eyes flicker at the flash of metal, and he grunts with pain. I take a package from the oilskin. "Here, I've brought some willow bark. It'll help the pain." I force the strip of willow between his teeth, then wash round the wound while he writhes. When I can see the injury clearly, I try to work out how his arm should lie. It is broken above the elbow, and the flesh is deeply cut and torn. I look at him, and he looks

67

back at me, then I dampen the willow bark with a palmful of water from the flagon and fit the curve of the wood to his tongue. He sucks, and closes his eyes. I stroke his hair, then grip his arm with both hands and straighten the bone. It is a blessing that his senses desert him again at this point, so that I can concentrate properly on fitting the bone together, unencumbered by his screams.

When the bone seems straight, I take a pot of Mother's elderberry, marigold and feverfew balm which I have brought, apply most of it to the wound, then splint the arm with a straight branch and tie it with the cloths I have used to clean him. He is shivering now, so I wrap him in my grey woollen cloak and take his own bloodstained clothing to wash in the beck. Watching the blood curl up into the water, I see again the line of Scots coming at me across the clearing, spreading out to enclose me, wearing draperies like this, and for a moment I am glad I hurt him. I spread his clothing on the brambles to dry, and return inside. He seems to have slipped into a more natural sleep now. He will have to make do with this bug-infested pallet for the time being, but when I return I shall bring blankets, a trussing-bed, more medication, bandages, a broom and fresh floor covering.

Chapter 8

I go back the next day, and the next. The Scot seems to have decided not to speak to me. He lies with his head turned away as I clean the hut, and him. His name is Robert. That much I have managed to drag out of him. He belongs to the Lacklies, one of the notorious border families against whom the queen herself has spoken out. I find a French rosary wound into his belt. One of the few times he speaks to me is when I put it into his hands. He looks at me doubtfully and says, "I'm grateful. Ye wouldnae be...?"

I shake my head. "No, but when you're well enough I'll get you across the bay to the monks at Cartmel."

A week goes by. The hovel is clean, and Robert is on a fresh straw and canvas trussing-bed, dressed in some of Father's cast-offs. He is a strange sight in these clothes which are old-fashioned and too short for him.

I am pleased with my handiwork in straightening his arm, and the bone shows signs of knitting, but the flesh itself hangs yellow and rotting, strings of it peeling away, and no herbs can mask its decaying smell. I bathe the wound daily, and am getting through a prodigious number of bandages. Once I have used them I have to burn them because of the state they are in.

Another week passes. Robert has bouts of delirium in which he raves in French and another language which I presume to be his own Scots tongue. He is too weak to stand, or even to turn himself over. I have to take the half hour's walk into the forest twice a day now, to tend him and dress his wound. I have used up the remaining ragged sheets which are kept for bandages in a chest next to the women's common room on the tower's east landing. The supply was depleted already after the battle. In desperation, late one night, I creep up to the linen press in the tiny room at the side of the living hall hearth, with my scissors concealed in my skirts. I can hear Father snoring in his room on the other side of the hearth. For once I wish he were out on the highway. I feel sick with guilt. This is a criminal act I am about to perform. Bedsheets are precious, and Mother is always so finicky about them. They have to be washed carefully, perfumed with lavender water, then pulled and snapped between her and Kate until they are straight, and folded with their corners and hems exactly right. Sheets are not just sheets; they are symbols of domestic decency.

I open the press. Layers of cream linen are stacked on deep shelves. I put my big copper candlestick on the floor and the flame streams in the draught. I move the candlestick along with my foot, and the scraping sound is very loud. Father coughs and stops snoring. I wait, then start to sort through the sheets, feeling for those which are smoothest for the Scotsman's arm. At last I pull a large one from the pile, and before I can lose my courage, hack into it. The scissors slew round on the thick material and wrench my hand. I gasp, pause, try again. I snick the hem; the tight double seam gives; there's no going back.

It's a large sheet, so I try to tear the main part, but it will not give. The material stretches, and tiny motes of linen rush up into the candlelight. I realise grimly that I am going to have to cut my way through every inch. With an increasingly sore hand, I ravage our precious bedlinen, for a Scot.

Part way through the week it occurs to me that Robert's angry silence may be caused by his being in a deep state of melancholy, so I mix borage oil into the broth which I feed him. It seems to help a little, when he is able to eat, which is not always. One day he says, "You're a bonny lass," which would have been laughably predictable under other circumstances, but which I take to be well meant. He would be bonny himself if he were not in such a sorry state. Meanwhile, his arm rots on him, and he is so

71

helpless that his limbs tremble when I move him. I fret, and have nightmares about him.

"Why do you raid us?" I ask, as he becomes more talkative. "Can't you breed your own cattle?"

"It isnae just for your cattle we come, Beatrice," he replies. "The cattle are just a wee little excuse. We want you destabilised, discontented down here in the border country with the law enforcement of your Protestant queen. We'll see good Queen Mary of Scots on the English throne yet."

I am outraged. "You make no secret of it then? It's well she is locked up, Scotsman."

He attempts to shrug his one shruggable shoulder. "Maybe ye'll let me die now."

The week after my raid on the linen press, I realise that I need more help. I shall have to consult a wise woman or doctor, without their realising my purpose. I know that Mother Bain, a wise woman and soothsayer, will be at the May Day fair in our neighbouring village, if only Robert can last until then.

He does. May Day dawns, and Verity and I stand on the battlements watching homesteaders with flowers in their hair appearing out of the mist and making their way past our tower, over the stony lea which borders the woods and on to the footpath which leads to the Old Corpse Road. It is nearly an hour's walk to Wraithwaite, part of it up a sheer limestone rockface with only a narrow, rough path cut into one of its deep clefts. Most of the May Day revellers are on foot, a few on horseback. A cart full of old women and young children wobbles by, taking the longer route round the edge of the woods.

"Oh rowan tree, oh rowan tree,
How sweet thou art to me.
I swear thou art the fairest bush
In all the north country,
Oh, rowan tree..."

Kate's pure, powerful voice rises up the tower walls as she leads my father's stallion into the barmkin. He must only just have arrived home. Verity takes off her cap and flings it at the beacon turret. "I fear there's a wagon to hell reserved for our father, Beatie."

We speak no more about him. It's a day for celebrating. We cannot set off just yet ourselves. It has become a tradition that our party from the tower arrives later. I think people probably feel we spoil their fun. As more revellers from the valley continue to drift past, Verity and I tour the battlements looking for damage caused by the Scots and discussing whether we need to send for the Irish builders who sometimes come over to do repairs.

I lean over, picking off bits of lard which have become hardened and brittle in the wind and rain, and consider telling Verity my secret. I feel a desperate need to share it with someone, but when I hear the anger in her voice towards the Scots, I realise I can tell no one, not even my sister.

Later we ride out from the tower with Hugh, Gerald, Germaine and James.

Hugh rides next to me, not speaking much. I think he is aggrieved that I have been neglecting him. Verity and Gerald ride behind, in even more profound silence. Soon Gerald drops back to ride with Germaine, and James Sorrell comes cantering up to join Verity. We pass large numbers of people walking. At the rockface we dismount and lead our horses up the steep, narrow path. Pebbles shoot from under the animals' hooves, and clang away down the valley. When we reach the top, Hugh takes Saint Hilda's reins and draws me to one side while we wait for the others.

"I may have to go away, Beatrice. You must not repeat this to anyone, but I wanted you to know." He takes hold of my hand.

"Away? Why?"

Germaine's and then Gerald's heads appear over the top of the rockface. Hugh bends towards me. "Cousin, our lords of Cumberland are planning a vengeance raid on the Scots, back over the border to burn their castles and houses. They're calling on the lords of Westmorland to rally men too, and join them. I'm bound to go. It's said the queen herself secretly supports it."

I stare at him, horrified. "Who else will go?" Hugh shrugs and helps Verity pull her horse over the top. When the others have joined us we remount and move on.

"Gerald will go," Hugh says as the others move ahead. "Father too, and your father will lead us, no doubt."

I stare ahead, chilled and frightened. We ride through pastures of flowering grasses whose polleny heads tremble in the heat haze. Blue harebells and maroon clover bloom amongst the rocks. Tufts of sheep's wool hang on brambles, and some homesteaders are collecting it to rub on their hands and faces. The countryside is peaceful and lovely, but I do not care. My thoughts are with Robert, my enemy, sick and alone in the hermit's cottage.

Chapter 9

Mother Bain is ancient and very wrinkled. Her grey linen cap hangs unstarched and askew about her ears. She has long, yellow nails. Her eyes are the colour of watery blue whey. She looks impossibly stooped and frail, seated in her little canvas booth away from the stalls and festivities. I have to queue for an hour to get in. While I wait, I watch children parading with flowers and singing May carols, and I wish I had their innocence and certainties.

"Aye, mistress?" Mother Bain wastes no time on polite greetings. Her voice creaks like an unoiled hinge. I try to find the right words, but feel suddenly overcome. The coolness of the booth and the close attention of the old woman undermine me, and I find my eyes stinging and tears coming. Mother Bain waits. She looks used to waiting. I understand why the queueing took so long.

I try to pull myself together. "I'm sorry, Mistress Bain. I need a healing potion."

"For yourself?"

"No... no, for a friend, a friend who has a wound, a serious wound that will not heal. The flesh is yellow and putrid. The bone is broken."

Her face remains impassive. "Aye." There is a long pause, during which I wonder if she is waiting for further explanation. Then she speaks with unexpected force. "You are deeply troubled, madam, and I see worse to come, though I cannot say what. I feel you have taken your own course, as has another close to you, and the result in both cases will be a death hunt. God help you."

I sit back, open-mouthed with horror.

She continues. "For your friend, take honey, water it by half from the holy well at Freewith, add spider webs from the hedgerow not the house, wind them round a silver spoon, as many as will cloud the liquid. Drop in the spoon and let it lie. Apply the potion every hour and cover with pounded comfrey leaves. Burn juniper branches close to the wound. Let your friend also chew stalks of boneset. That is all."

"Thank you. Thank you, mistress," I stammer, and repeat the instructions to be sure I have them right. I open the purse at my waist. "I am grateful. How much do I owe you?"

She sighs. "I would rather not charge you, lady. You have troubles, and worse to come, but I must live and eat. One shilling."

It is expensive, but I do not begrudge it. If the potion works, then Robert might not lose his arm. As it is at the moment, I fear the day when he will ask me to cut it off for him. We both know that the rot could spread until it kills him, and do it myself I would have to, because nobody else could be trusted to help a Scot. As if reading my thoughts, the old woman shoots out her hand and grasps my skirt. "Where is the wound?"

"On his arm, above the elbow."

"If it is too late, if the bayne I have prescribed can no longer cure it, then you must send for the Cockleshell Man."

My skin shrivels with dismay. I know I could never ask for help from the Cockleshell Man, nor from anyone else for that matter. I put the silver coin into the old woman's hand and rise to my feet, but Mother Bain does not let go of me.

"It is not too late to turn aside," she whispers. "You can save yourself, child."

I press my hand over hers. "I know. Thank you. I cannot. What will happen? Do you know?"

She sinks back on her stool and releases her grip on my skirt. "Nay. It is hidden, and well so, I fear. God bless you."

I leave the tent, certain that this time she was lying.

My legs are shaking when I rejoin Hugh, who is watching the bear-baiting in the pit by the tavern. I also stand and watch for a moment. The bear and the bandog seem evenly matched. The dog is nimble but the bear is knowing, his little pink eyes watchful. When the dog seizes him by the throat, he claws at its head. They roar and toss and tumble, shaking their ears. Blood and saliva whirl about their heads. I have never liked bear-baiting, but today I feel disgusted, and move away to watch the maypole dancing instead. Minstrels are playing a jig while young girls and boys dance round, weaving the ribbons into patterns. The pole has begun to tilt ominously towards the crowd. Some members of the crowd have begun tilting ominously too, after numerous visits to the tavern and ale wagon.

In front of the parsonage at the far side of the green, a group of moorish dancers are performing to music which clashes with that of the maypole minstrels. Further off, at the edge of the wood, an archery contest is taking place. As aim starts to deteriorate, I fear for the wellbeing of the onlookers.

On an improvised stage by the ale wagon the masque of Robin and Marion is being enacted, but none of the travelling players seems to know the words, and one keeps falling off the stage into the audience. It is difficult to know which entertainment to patronise first. Young men and women, some from our valley, are taking over the maypole from the boys and girls now, and I saunter over to join them. The day is growing hotter, and people are throwing off shawls, caps and jerkins, and in some cases removing even more basic items of clothing. Several shirtless men have begun a fight outside the church. The wagon loaded with barrels of ale is dragged a little closer to the maypole by two hefty farm lads, and its fermented smell wafts ahead of it. A yokel, capering foolishly in a woman's fustian gown, his ruddy face unshaven, thrusts a mug of ale at me. I gasp as it slops down my bodice, then laugh and drink it down. It is the most carefree I have felt all day.

"Eee lass, I'll fetcher another." The yokel seems to have taken a fancy to me, so I excuse myself and go to look for Hugh and the rest of our party. On the way here, Verity galloped ahead of us, her hair streaming out behind her, her hat used to flog her horse, rejecting the rest of us and our staid progress. I have only caught glimpses of her since. On one occasion I saw her with Gerald at the pedlar's stall. He seemed to be buying her a roll of red silk, though looking very grim about it. It is increasingly difficult to imagine them wed.

Suddenly I see an astonishing sight, my Cousin Gerald arm in arm with Germaine. They are doing some sort of ridiculous kicking dance to the music, trying to keep time, laughing into each other's faces and nearly falling over. I stare. Germaine is supposed to be helping Kate sell our woollen cloth on a stall at the edge of the green. Hugh appears beside me. I grasp him by the arm and point. "Hugh, look at that."

He drapes his arm across my shoulders. "Oh dear. They're getting careless."

"What do you mean?"

He sighs. "Beatie, a lot goes on in our homes that is better not known."

"Well I think you had better tell me, since Gerald is supposed to marry my sister."

Hugh watches them for a moment. "I suppose you might as well know. There are worse things, despite what Parson Becker might say." He sounds hard and uncaring. "Gerald loves Germaine, no matter that she is well nigh twice his age, and I think she loves him too. She stays in the service of your father because she has nowhere else to go. Obviously she can't come to us. Mother would never allow it. They can't have a future together, so they make the most of the present. You can see how they are." He sounds a little wistful, but adds, "They are to be pitied."

The music is speeding up. It adds to my sense of unreality. Germaine, awful Germaine, with my cousin: it is beyond scandal. It is unthinkable. I turn away from them and take Hugh by the hand and say to him, "Let's dance." I pull him into the stumbling circle of people who are grasping hands round the maypole. The ribbons have long been abandoned in a hopeless tangle. Everyone is laughing and trying to start moving in unison. Little by little we begin to gallop sideways, propelled by the momentum of those who started first and have gained speed. The music takes on an edge of wildness. The ale I have drunk whistles in my head, and I feel I am dancing to a different tune from everyone else. I fall over and roll away, out of the circle.

I lie on the grass for several minutes, terribly hot, and unlace the top of my bodice with one hand. I seem to have ended up under the big oak tree in the centre of the green, where several other people are also cooling off. Hugh has been carried away by the maypole dance. Suddenly Germaine is looming above me. She stands looking down, her dark eyes observing my unlaced bodice.

"Beatrice, I think it's time to go home. I do not think your mother would be pleased to see you lying here half unclothed." She says it without any convincing air of authority. Germaine did once have authority over us, when she was our teacher of music and needlework, but since she has tried to inveigle herself into Father's affections, and since Verity and I have grown up, the balance of power has changed.

I sit up, bemused by my new knowledge of her. "Germaine, you were supposed to be helping Kate on the stall," is all I can find to say.

She smiles. "Kate manages well enough. Where is Master Hugh? Is he not looking after you properly?"

I heave myself to my feet. Hugh reappears, red-faced and out of breath, making a reply unnecessary. Instead I enquire, "And where is Master Gerald, my dear Germaine?"

"Gerald is watching the cockfight, Beatrice." She looks unutterably bored with me, and turns her attention to Hugh. "Perhaps Master Hugh would like to go and join him for half an hour before we go home." She gestures to where the sun is sliding rooster-red into the trees. It is a dismissal. I am almost speechless at her effrontery.

Hugh hesitates. "I'll go and buy some sweetmeats," he offers, and moves away with a backward glance over his shoulder at me. I pull a face at him, and he pulls one back.

Germaine gives an exasperated sigh. "You silly young things may act superior. I envy you your childish ignorance." She shakes her head. "I live in the real world, Beatrice, where poverty and loneliness lie in wait for you at every turn. I just want to warn you, if you tell your father about Gerald and me, it is at your own peril. There are things I can tell about you, too."

I step back. "Whatever do you mean, Germaine? You have nothing to hold over me."

Germaine smooths back her thick, brown hair with both hands. "Nay, mistress? Nothing in the woods?"

For a moment I feel quite ill. Then I tell myself she cannot know anything for sure. I have been so careful. I put on an expression of bewilderment. Germaine places her hand on her hip and tilts her head, as if assessing my performance. "Don't fret, *my dear Beatrice*." She parodies my earlier, aloof tone. "Your secret is safe with me, so long as mine is safe with you. We all have secrets, you, me, your father, your mother..."

I stare at her, angry and puzzled. "What do you mean, my mother?"

Hugh is coming back, laden with marchpane and honeycakes. Germaine studies the drifts of bright-edged cloud visible between the branches of the oak tree. "It will rain, don't you think, before the day is out?" She lowers her gaze. "Your mother? Oh, it is her business. Beatrice, I wish you were that good child I once knew, and not of an age to have secret lovers, but if you are so grown up, then you must be truly grown up, and not make such a fuss about things."

I feel almost sick with relief. A secret lover. All she thinks I have is a secret lover? I want to laugh. As we all ride home together the long way round, stopping at the holy well on the edge of Freewith, I know that I must be more careful than ever now. Germaine is watching me. I must be vigilant, and leave no trail, no clues, which might lead her to Robert. If she were to find out that my secret was not a secret lover but a secret Scotsman, then I fear there would be no means of shutting her mouth.

On the way we pass Parson Becker, pale and dark-haired on his tall black horse. He raises his hand in greeting but does not smile. Once, this chance meeting would have fuelled my imagination for weeks. Now, I cannot think about him, because he symbolises the things from which my involvement with Robert has excluded me: honesty and truth, and more than anything, loyalty to the people amongst whom I live.

Chapter 10

The remedy is brewed, the comfrey leaves pounded to a poultice, the juniper branches and stalks of boneset in my saddlebag. Everyone is drinking milkthistle this morning, and swearing never to touch ale again. I collect spiders' webs from the wild raspberry canes on the Pike during my morning watch, and set off into the forest straight after.

When I arrive at the cottage I find Robert standing behind the door. I jump back. "Robert, you frightened the life out of me!"

His face has its usual unhealthy sheen. His eyes are dull like boiled shellfish. He is propping himself against the doorframe. He is taller than I thought. I look up at him. "Robert, you are not fit to be on your feet. Get back into bed at once."

He reaches out with his one good arm. I realise that he

is stuck. I put my arms round him and take his weight. His fingernails scratch my wrist, and I wonder why I have not thought to cut them. I must shave him again too. He is so young, little more than my own age, with just a scattering of honey-coloured stubble, but it is more obvious now that he is standing up. I fit my shoulder under his arm and totter him to the bed. He is almost unmanageably heavy. His head rolls against the top of mine, and I wonder unworthily what small creatures from the floor might have taken up residence there. As we stop to rest he mutters, "Beatrice, my arm. The infection is spreading. It will kill me. Please, you must take it off."

As if the words have drained him, his knees buckle. I ease him on to the bed.

"Lie down. Lean back." I prop him against the roll of sheepskin at the head of the bed. "Robert, I have a new bayne to save your arm." I pull up his grey blanket and support his arm on a log which I have padded with wool and linen. He has half torn off his dressings, so now I remove them completely. The wound looks no better, and smells foul. All his joints show a puffiness. I surround the injury with linen, then slop Mother Bain's remedy in.

"Hah!" His breath is indrawn sharply. The mixture oozes into the torn flesh then drips away past the splint. At the same time a solitary tear seeps past Robert's eyelashes. I smooth his clammy hair.

"I have a treat for you, Robert," I tell him. I bind the comfrey poultice in place, then light the juniper branches in the doorway, and step out over them. I fetch a small earthenware bottle from my saddlebag. "It's a sort of Scottish wine spirit called..." I peer at the name inked on the leather-covered stopper. "... usquebaugh? Do you know it? I spent a fortnight's wool money on it at the May fair." I ease out the stopper and sniff. The fumes knock me back. Robert stares at it in wonder, then takes it from my hand and puts it to his mouth. He chokes, coughs, gasps for breath, then holds it out to me.

"Try it. It's whiskybae." He corrects my pronunciation. A scarlet flush is spreading up his neck.

I shake my head. "No thanks." I restopper the bottle. "I brought it for you. Have the rest later. It seems rather strong."

With no more comment Robert retrieves the bottle from my hand, removes the stopper with his teeth and drinks the rest of it. Then he sags against the log, curling protectively round his arm, a blank look of despair replacing the raw agony on his face.

"You do a lot for an enemy," he says to me tiredly. I stay with him until he has gone to sleep.

May draws on. The woods are veined with bluebells. Their devastating blueness is like something forbidden, too wild and intense for respectable people. One day after leaving Robert I lie down in a hollow of the woods where bluebells cover every bit of ground. Their sappy scent fills the air. Their drooping, delicate bells feel cool and taut against my bare arms. I lie there realising that I think of nothing but Robert these days. Hugh, my future husband, rarely crosses my mind. I should be worrying about the danger he will be in when the men march on Scotland. Instead I worry only about the added danger to Robert, as anti-Scottish feeling rises.

I seem to be falling out with everybody, particularly with Germaine, who apparently thinks we have a mutual conspiracy going between us. She looks at me from under her eyebrows and makes demands she would not normally have dared. I watch her with my father – Mother is scarcely home these days – and wonder how a household can have gone so comprehensively wrong.

It is a humid spring, heat and dampness alternating with wind and rain. One sultry morning, with dawn coming up behind the hills and storm clouds rolling in across the bay, after I have stayed most of the night listening to Robert's delirium, I accept that the treatment has not worked, and is not going to.

Robert has become unbearable. Even when in possession of his senses, he is always angry with me, calling me a heathen, and daring me to hand him over to the authorities, after having hidden him for so long. There are border laws against even speaking to Scots, and I have done far worse. He knows I cannot betray him now. The infection has stabilised with Mother Bain's potion, but has not lessened, and Robert weakens daily, as fevers flash through his blood.

So, this hot, damp dawn, I stand wearily outside the cottage and consider how to go about taking an arm off. I am hoping that my overnight absence from the tower has not been noticed, and that those at home will merely assume I have risen early. The first rays of sun catch the morning mist and the tree trunks glow opalescent. There is a rustle to the side of me in the hazel thicket. It is a young red deer eating the cobnuts which have scarcely begun to grow on the branches yet. It looks at me but does not move away. If Hugh or Gerald had been here, with the stink of long-gone stag hunts in their hair, it would have fled. For some reason its acceptance of me gives me the strength to go back inside and say, "Robert, your arm, I don't think it can be saved."

The skin is peeling from his lips. His mouth moves stiffly, like that of the ventriloquist at the May fair. He whispers, "I know. Thank you. You've tried, Beatrice."

I go back outside. I would rather he did not see me in tears. The deer is still there. It moves a little closer. We stare at one another. The sky brightens and shadows sharp as knife blades section up the clearing. Young hazel leaves rip and rustle as the deer tongues them into its mouth. Birdsong fills the woods, far into the distance. Slowly I calm myself, and accept that I cannot cut off Robert's arm myself. It is beyond me.

"Robert." I go and kneel down beside him. "I can't take your arm off. I'll have to get someone else to do it."

"If you call the doctor then you and I will both hang."

89

"You'd hang. I'd burn. That's what they do to women traitors."

He turns his head away. "Who owes you a favour? Whose mouth can ye shut?"

"There is someone who'll do it and maybe not talk. Not someone who owes me a favour, but a sawbones called the Cockleshell Man. He's a bit of an outsider himself, so perhaps won't be as bound by the law as the rest of us. Anyway, if you remain silent, he might just assume you're a hermit like the last one." I stroke Robert's damp face, and he winces, as if all his flesh were a wound. I walk back to the tower to saddle Saint Hilda.

People say many things about the Cockleshell Man. I try not to think about them as I ride through the clifftop woods towards Mere Point. He does the jobs which no one else will do, hacking off diseased limbs and pulling out rotten teeth, but people say he also casts spells, and that he has a secret tunnel from his cottage on the clifftop to one of the caves in the cliff face, where he conducts his magic. Certainly no one goes near that cave, for fear of meeting the Cockleshell Man lurking at the back.

It is necessary to pass my cousins' tower in order to reach the crofter's cottage where the Cockleshell Man lives, so I call on my aunt to give myself an excuse for being over this way. Gerald is standing watch on the battlements. I wave to him and he blows me a kiss.

This tower is more elegant than ours. It has decorative triple-arched windows with golden sandstone lintels and mullions, as well as the usual arrow slits. Some of the windows have beautiful painted glass in them, and there are stone carvings over the door and around the battlements. I consider that really I should not mind living here with Hugh, and that surely firm friendship and a shared sense of humour are as good a basis for marriage as I am likely to find in the Westmorland hills. Yet somehow, today, the idea seems even more ludicrous than ever.

Aunt Juniper comes to the door as I arrive. "Good morning, Beatrice. Hugh is on watch on Beacon Hill. Do you want to go up and join him?"

We exchange kisses. "Good morning, Auntie. I may go up that way later."

She looks pleased. She does most of the matchmaking in the district, and I suspect she finds it frustrating that her nearest relatives are turning out to be most resistant to her plans. She leads the way into the kitchen where she is burning young bracken to make soap. Its eye-watering smell hangs in the room.

"Here, you can pound lime for the soap while we talk." She passes me a mortar of limestone already fired and crumbling. "I wish Gerald and Verity thought as much of each other as you and Hugh do," she adds. "Verity seems to drive Gerald away. Can you not speak to her about it, Niece?"

I sit down at the long elm table. I am not in the mood to be tactful. I take up the pestle to pound the limestone and reply, "Auntie... Verity does not want to marry

Gerald. To be honest I don't think she wants to marry anyone. She likes to do things her own way, and she thinks Gerald would be like my father, and interfere."

My aunt looks at me, astonished, across the rank-smelling ashes of bracken. "But it is all settled. She and Gerald must have one of the towers. What other possible arrangement could there be?"

I sigh, and gaze away towards the high windows in the upper storey of the kitchen, where a gallery runs round and doves are crooning among the rafters. "I don't know, Auntie," is all I can reply.

On my way out I pass the hunched figure of Uncle Juniper, and he hugs and kisses me and tells me in bloodthirsty detail how his fighting dogs are doing. By the time I remount Saint Hilda and ride off across the springy turf towards the clifftop path, my nerves are in a worse state than ever.

Chapter 11

The tiny cottage of the Cockleshell Man is half hidden in woodland near the edge of the cliff. I tether Saint Hilda to a tree and walk up the path between beds of medicinal herbs. On either side of his door stand crams, long rakes with which he scrapes cockles out of the sand. Valerian, the vile-smelling phew plant, is growing by the wall. When there is no reply to my first knock I break off one of its bright pink flowers, smack it against the wall to remove insects, and suck its revolting juices to soothe away my panic.

I knock again, my stomach turning with fear. What person in their right mind comes to the door of the Cockleshell Man? Yet, after a while, when the door opens, he stands there on the threshold like any man. He is tall and broad-shouldered. His face is encased in thick, light-brown hair and a beard. He looks as if he has just woken up. His expression is wary.

"Aye?" His small grey eyes stare at me. His clothes reek of fish and salt water. I step nervously back and almost fall over a sack of cockles beside the path.

"Come you in," he says abruptly, and turns to lead the way into his dark house. "I see it isn't cockles you've come for, since you see fit to trample all over them." He smiles, and I realise this was meant to be a joke. "What is it? Are you afraid of me?"

I nod. His face seems to redden, though in the dimness it is difficult to tell. I say, "I've come to ask you a favour."

"Oh?" He indicates that I should sit down on a bale of straw by the window.

Chaff leaks out and hovers in the light as I seat myself and arrange my skirts.

"I know you act as a sawbones," I say to him.

He frowns. "Aye. I butcher the unfortunate." His large hands clench and unclench, as if already hefting axe and saw, and I begin to feel rather faint.

"There's a man with an injured arm, sir. It will not heal. The infection is threatening to spread and kill him."

He nods. "Who might this man be?"

I suddenly notice something astonishing. Draped across the rough table in the corner is an embroidered shawl woven in lilac silk and wool, and patterned with cream lilies. I know it very well. I embroidered it myself as a gift for my mother two Christmases ago. I stare at the shawl, and I stare at the Cockleshell Man, and I do not answer his question. Instead I say, "Sir, I don't know your real name, but I'm Beatrice Garth of Barrowbeck Tower."

The look of shock is there and gone. He too glances at the shawl, then back at me. I ask him, "Do you know my mother?" It's possible of course that my mother has had treatment from him, and paid with the shawl, but I don't think so. She would have paid in silver, or cheese, or mutton, or sheepskin. She would not have given away a garment I had spent weeks making for her. I wait for his reply, trying to stifle my feeling of disbelief, to make sense of things.

He crosses to the door and closes it, his head half turned away from me, and says, "I am acquainted with her."

I rub my hands across my face and ask, "Do you want me to return that shawl to her?"

He emerges from the shadows. A beam of sunlight shines on the filmy surface of his jerkin, showing up the blue-green glister of fish scales. He shakes his head. "Nay. I thank you. She'll come and get it herself."

Behind the shock of discovering that my mother appears to visit this man, is something else, an awareness that here is someone whose mouth I really can shut, someone who needs my silence as much as I need his, someone who would be murdered in his bed if my father were to find out what I have just found out, no matter how innocent it might be.

95

I look up at him. "I hope I can rely on your silence if I tell you that... the man with the injury is a Scot."

The Cockleshell Man's eyes widen briefly. "Is he indeed." He laughs. "You're your mother's daughter all right."

The notion that I am trying to pressurise him doesn't appear to have occurred to him. He asks, "Is he in much pain, yon Scot?"

I glance over my shoulder, jittery that even indoors such a word should be said. "Yes, terrible pain."

"Then there's no time to waste. There are things I need to collect. You can wait here for me." He opens the door and strides out, leaving it swinging behind him. I run after him.

"Wait! Where are you going?"

He is heading into the clifftop woods, his stiff breeches cracking and flapping. "I'm going to find some little friends who'll help me," he calls back over his shoulder. "You'll not like 'em, lass."

I cringe. What can he mean? Elves and goblins? Whatever have I started? I cross myself, a Popish habit for which Father would have beaten me.

When the Cockleshell Man returns there are no elves or goblins with him, only a small leather bag hung at his waist. He seems relieved to find me still there, and I realise he thought I might not have waited. I wonder how often the Cockleshell Man finds that people have not waited. He opens a chest next to the hearth and withdraws a serrated metal saw with a bone handle at each end, and also a bone-handled knife. He hangs these from his waist with the small leather bag. I support myself on the window frame, feeling sick. He looks at me. "You can help me, Beatrice Garth. Take down the third jar from the left, on that shelf over the door, and count out twenty seeds into this." He hands me a beechwood mortar and pestle. "He'll not feel the knife, if we do have to cut him."

I take down the jar and count out twenty tiny black seeds. "What are they?" I ask.

"Henbane. Do you have an interest in medicine?"

I shake my head. He smiles. "He may sleep for two days, but he'll be healing all the while." He grinds the seeds together with an expert flick of the wrist, then tips them into a fold of parchment. "Show me the way then."

We cut over the slope of Beacon Hill. I keep Saint Hilda to a walk while the Cockleshell Man strides behind me. Every time I come to the hermit's cottage I am afraid of finding Robert dead. I sniff as I tether Saint Hilda by the door. I can smell his arm from here.

"Robert?" He is lying under the blanket as I left him. He half opens his eyes. They are bloodshot and vacant. "Robert, I've brought a healer to help you."

"Aye." He glances at the surgical instruments which are catching the sunshine in the doorway, and closes his eyes again.

We remove the bandages, easing them away with water from the beck, until just the splint and tapes remain on Robert's arm. Yellow pus oozes out over the splint.

The flesh is rainbow colours from purple to green.

"Did you set this bone?" the Cockleshell Man asks.

I nod. "It was a long time ago."

"You did well. We'll not have to chop off your handiwork, Beatrice, God willing." He removes the leather bag from his waist and glances at me. "I could tell you to go, but you clearly have a talent for healing. This bone is well nigh mended. I could teach you. Do you want to learn some of the old ways that nature clears up putrefaction? You need a strong stomach."

I have no idea what he means, but I am flattered that he praised my bone setting, so I answer, "Yes please. Show me."

For a moment he hesitates, as if still doubting my stamina, then he upends the leather bag over a woollen cloth and pours out a stream of maggots.

I rock back on my heels. "Dear God."

The Cockleshell Man is shaping the woollen cloth in his hands, easing the maggots into the centre, then he quickly applies it to Robert's arm. "They work for infected ears too," he informs me, glancing over to the far side of the room where I have retreated. "You just tip them in. Wash them out with salt water two days later." He finishes tying bandages round the cloth, then supports the arm in a sling. He stands up. "I'll come back tomorrow. Bring him wine and turnip broth this evening. No meat. No milk." He walks out, his unused saw and knife swinging at his belt. On the trussing-bed Robert lies silent and unmoving, his eyes shut.

I scarcely sleep that night. When I do, maggots seethe in my dreams. Robert would not touch the broth and wine which I took him after my watch on the Pike. I could not stop looking at his arm in its sling, and my own skin screamed with horror. When I left him, it was very late, and the woods were completely dark. Robert seemed too vulnerable to be left alone. It felt like a night of evil, a night when such men as my father ride out.

It seems my father did indeed ride out last night, since Germaine is wearing a shockingly vulgar emerald brooch on her dress this morning. Verity, whom I have scarcely seen for days, informs her at morning prayers that green is simply not her colour, and for the first time Germaine seems on the verge of tears. She turns away. I realise she looks as tired as I feel. I do not brush her off when she asks if she can exchange her watch on Beacon Hill this afternoon with mine this morning. I know it is so that she can meet Gerald. In fact it suits me very well, because it means I can set off early for my appointment at the hermit's cottage.

When I arrive, I find that the Cockleshell Man has been there half the night. He is lying under the window where the oiled cloth flaps in the chilly breeze. He says, "You're just in time. We're going to take a look at it now, aren't we, Robert."

I step over the threshold into the half-light. There is more alertness in Robert's eyes than I have seen since I toppled him from the tower window. Together, the Cockleshell Man and I unbind the arm. The difference is apparent at once. Beyond the visual shockingness of the infestation, the flesh is swollen and puckered, and red shows where it was yellow before. The maggots are eating the poison. "Two more days," says the Cockleshell Man. "We'll check it again tomorrow. He'll not be fit to move, to wash them off in the sea, so mebbe bring a block of salt, Beatrice, and we'll use water from the beck."

He walks with me to the door. "He'll be fit to move by Allhallows, and home before winter sets in. I'll guide him over the sands when the time comes."

"Cedric." We both turn. Robert is struggling to sit up.

"So you have a name." I smile at the Cockleshell Man. He grins and turns to Robert. "Aye?"

"I've nothing to pay you with."

Cedric, the Cockleshell Man, concentrates on folding up the used dressings he is taking away with him. "It'll not tek much imagination to know how you can pay, Robert," he says, "you and your kin. If you're in any doubt, then I daresay Mistress Beatrice will enlighten you."

Robert lies back down, watching us. Cedric and I stand outside the doorway. Fish scales are shining in his beard today, and he really does not smell so good. "Master Cedric..."

"Cedric."

"Cedric, I'm so grateful to you. I must pay you on Robert's behalf."

"Thank you, Beatrice, but nay, there's no call for that." He goes to step over the broken wall. I put out a hand to stop him.

"My mother…" I hesitate. He doesn't help me. "Can you just tell me… the reason she comes to visit you… it isn't because she's ill, is it?"

He pauses, one foot up on the wall. "No, she's not ill." He stares at me for a moment, then he says, "Beatrice, be careful of yon Scot. It would be even worse than loving a Cockleshell Man, that would." Then he steps over the wall and walks off into the forest.

I can pretend not to understand his warning – the idea of course is ridiculous – but this is not a day for pretence. My thoughts have centred round Robert for weeks. The improvement in him makes me feel physically lighter, as if his diseased arm had been a burden across my shoulders. I am glad he will recover, and, I tell myself firmly, I shall be glad when he is gone.

As for the strange and mysterious association between Cedric and my mother, that is something I shall think about later. I go back into the cottage. Robert speaks before I can. "I'd not have come raiding here again anyhow, Beatrice," he says. "You know that, don't you. Not now that I know you're here."

I start to clear up the wooden bowl of water and the washing cloths. "I suppose you mean you'll just stick to raiding other places then. Is that it?" I ask. I cannot help my hostile tone, or tell whether it is in response to the Cockleshell Man's warning.

Robert moves his injured arm. "Some things are out of my control, Beatrice."

"So is this to be our last raid then, here at Barrowbeck?"

"As far as my people are concerned, once they hear about what you've done, I'm sure it will be, but there are plenty more along the border, the Armstrongs and Elliots, the Irvines and Trotters and Johnstones and the rest. I cannae answer for them. They're a rough lot."

"You're a rough lot, Robert," I tell him.

He smiles. It is such a shock. I realise I have never seen him smile before. He is suddenly human, real, a person with warmth in his eyes. I turn away.

He adds, "A lot may depend on whether you Englishmen come raiding us in the meantime."

I think of the lords of Westmorland and Cumberland, and I am afraid.

Within a week the flesh of Robert's arm is pink, and puckering into healthy scabs. Within a fortnight it is healing over, and he can stand unaided.

Chapter 12

We are always on edge for months after a raid. There are the obvious physical depredations to repair – houses burnt and needing rebuilding, temporary shelters to be constructed to tide the homesteaders over – but there's also the grief and shock and lost sense of security. That we ever felt secure is odd, since the constant keeping of watch implies a lack of security, but you can't live in fear all the time. You forget; you fool yourself. You would go mad otherwise.

So as the weather grows warmer, the raid recedes into merely a bad memory. In the valley the grain grows tall, and our long-horned black cattle and flock of white-faced horned sheep grow fat on good pastures. Yet I feel distanced from the farm, my family, my household duties. I can see that my mother is puzzled by me, though not as puzzled as I am by her. I find myself watching her covertly. The shawl reappears in her bedchamber. She is charming but distant towards Father, abstracted round the house and dairy, often away. I find it impossible to imagine that she has more than just a friendship with the Cockleshell Man. They are both interested in healing, after all, so it would make sense. Yet at thirty-three she looks ten years younger, too young to be trapped with my father, and the secrecy which she and Cedric maintain would seem to suggest a possibility which I'd rather not consider.

I feel that my normal life has been escaping from me while I have been concentrating on Robert. Things on the farm feel unfamiliar because I have spent so much time at the cottage, and even when I am not there, I am thinking about it. Robert's improvement progresses along with the improvement in the weather, as spring turns to summer. I make a decision to visit him less often. He can heal just as well on his own. I go alternate days, then every third day, and take him enough food to last. The days I do not go I spend down in the valley, helping the homesteaders rebuild the houses which Robert and his companions destroyed.

Robert makes occasional wobbly-kneed forays into the forest himself, and sometimes kills and roasts a squirrel or rabbit. On the days when I don't go, I feel as if the forest itself is calling me back, the raw smell of the beechwoods, the golden-brown mutter of the beck, the idea of Robert, gathering in my head, then Robert himself waiting for me, his eyes bright and his hair damp from his habit of lying in the water and letting it stream over him.

One hot morning when I do not go, travelling shearers arrive at our farm. We have been timing their progress northwards from Lancaster, so we are ready for them. The two men, brown and thin, set to work in the barmkin, and I go down to watch their impressive skills in action. I climb to the top of the barmkin wall and sit with the sun burning on my back. The men's short, pointed shears flash in the light, moving with unsettling speed. The men strip sheep after sheep, the animals held firmly between their knees. These men are known to be daring and improper, given half a chance. Girls in the valley are warned against them. As I sit there, one of them stands up to stretch his back, then comes over to me and takes hold of my ankle with both hands, as if to pull me off the wall. His hands are stained dark by oil from the fleeces, and are soft as courtiers' hands, with tiny cuts along the sides of his index fingers, from thorns in the wool. He smiles up at me. I look back down at him and say, "I'm the one who'll be paying you, Master Shearer. Or not, as the case may be."

He removes his hands from my ankle in a slow, deliberate caress, murmuring, "Well, lady, there'll be no extra charge for this," before returning to his work.

I lean back, propped with my hands behind me on the wall, and raise my face to the sun. The stones are warm, and rough with lichen under my palms. On the slope, insects buzz in the heather and bracken. I can feel my bones and muscles loosening in the heat. Suddenly there is a voice behind me.

"Beatie?"

I turn my head, startled. It is Parson Becker standing below, with his lightweight black summer robes hitched up round his middle with a piece of rope for ease of riding. "I brought you some books," he says. "The ones I mentioned on Sunday. Don't get down. I'll come up and join you."

I reach down to help him. "Those clothes aren't meant for climbing walls in, Parson," I tell him.

He smiles and loosens his collar, and scrambles up beside me without my help. "I've left the books in the gatehouse for you."

Verity and I are amazingly well educated for girls. Mother said that if the queen could learn Latin, Greek and Italian, then so could we. We used to ride through the woods to Wraithwaite twice a week to be taught by old Parson Pattinson. He was always very strict and angry with us at first – he was only used to teaching boys – but later his attitude changed, and he spent many more hours with us than Father ever paid him for. When Parson Pattinson died and young Parson Becker took over our education, I wasted many a long afternoon admiring this beautiful new priest, barely hearing a word of what he said. I glance at him now, and wonder if he ever realised.

"I'm supposed to come and talk to you about marrying

Hugh," he says. I stare at him in alarm. This seems deeply unfair of Aunt Juniper. I feel angry. He sees my expression and pulls a face and says, "It's simply that you and Verity both appear slow... unwilling even... to become formally betrothed to your cousins. That's all. No one's talking about setting a date for the weddings yet."

I hunch my shoulders forward and stare at the shearers. "Betrothal is so final, sir." I decide to be formal, to punish him; I know he values the informal friendship which has grown out of our lessons. "Verity and I are both needed here at the tower still. We're really not ready to think about rearranging the households yet."

"Or is it perhaps that neither of you really wants to?" John Becker asks.

I gaze at him. "Is that relevant?"

He reaches out, and with unusual hesitancy for him, takes hold of my hand. "There's plenty of time," he says. "I've said what I was supposed to say. Now we can talk about something more interesting."

We do not talk about anything more interesting. I look down at his hand, and reflect that he would not be making this fatherly gesture if he knew the thoughts I have sometimes harboured about him. The shearer who held my ankle whistles at us, and John laughs and lets go, then we watch the shearers in silence. Fine strands of wool drift by, and the oily smell of cut wool is in the air. The shearers' tempered steel blades stab the sheep's fine under-fur with speed and deftness, making the heavy outer coats peel elegantly away. One by one whole fleeces are thumped on to the slatted table, outer side up, to have the scraggings, the tail area with its dried droppings, pulled off and thrown away by Leo's son, Dickon. He then eases away the inferior wool at the sides of the fleece and throws it into a basket. The top quality wool from the sheep's backs is thrown into another basket.

Women from the village come and go in relays, carrying the fleeces to the beck to be rubbed with foamweed and rinsed clean. Men from the village move the sheep round the barmkin in an orderly manner, so that those waiting to be shorn are ready, and those already shorn are out of the way. Despite the bustle and the constant calling of the sheep, the scene is tranquil and self-contained, like the man next to me. The gentle wrestling of the amber-eyed animals, the soft mist of fine wool drifting on to our clothes, the stillness of John Becker, create a sense of peace in me, a feeling I had forgotten over recent months.

A bee blunders into the lace of my cap. I jerk back and shake my head, trying to dislodge it. John pulls my hair loose and shakes the bee free.

"Thank you." We look at each other. "I have to go and get new baskets for the fleeces," I say awkwardly, and tuck my hair back in. He nods. I swing my legs over the wall, and jump down, my face hot, and all around me the bees lose their stings and fade to burn marks on the heather.

Later John helps me organise the long tables in the

meadow ready for the shearing feast at the end of the day. Aunt Juniper arrives and says, "You've got the parson shifting furniture? Good. I like to see a bit of humility in a priest."

In the kitchen, when I am carrying out the beasting tarts to the tables, I ask her, "Who are you going to marry Parson Becker to, Auntie?"

She looks mildly shocked. "I daresay that one will please himself whom he marries." She bites into one of the rich yellow tarts made from the milk of young cows who have newly calved this year, and licks the sweet custard off her fingers, ignoring Kate's possessive glare. "Why, Niece? Do you have a suggestion?"

I shake my head, and go back outside, to where John is talking to our neighbours, and stand with him and watch the sun sink butter-yellow into the sea.

That night I dream John Becker is shearing sheep. The blades flash and snap, and I watch as if in a trance. Then suddenly they slip and gash his upper arm horribly. I spring forward to help him, and for a moment he and Robert are the same person in my dream, but the shock has half woken me, and the image fades into the uncertain light of dawn. After a while I get up and pull on yesterday's work clothes, pack some left-over beasting tarts into waxed cloth and follow my usual path through the forest.

Robert is sitting sideways on the trussing-bed when I reach the cottage. I have told him he must pretend to be dumb if anyone comes here. Now he teases me by mouthing, "Greetings, Beatrice." I unwrap the food. He says, "You're dressed like a peasant today."

I look at him, clad in tattered breeches, ragged green jerkin and patched linen shirt, and reply, "Well, you look utterly elegant, my dear."

"Where did you put my weapons, Beatrice?" he asks as we eat the beasting tarts. They seem very rich for so early in the day, and I reflect that this is just another sign of my general moral decline.

"I threw them into Mistholme Moss," I answer him.

"What?" He looks incredulous. "I thought you said you'd buried them somewhere."

"That was your clothes. No Robert, your weapons are at the bottom of a bog."

I watch his despair, and for a moment I feel it myself. He is a person to me now, not just something to be repaired. I lick my fingers and lean towards him. "Let me see your arm. How does it feel today?"

He watches me push up his sleeve and remove the bandages. His flesh is almost healed, though extensively marked with deep red scars. I smile at him. "This really is better, isn't it. We'll leave these off today. You just need to get your strength back now."

Suddenly, instead of me crouching over him, he is crouching over me. I draw back into the herbs and straw of the floor covering. He makes no move to readjust the distance between us. Slowly I relax. He stands up, no longer trembling when he tries to make his limbs support him. "Aye, you're right. I have to get my strength back. I must start walking and running and lifting. I'll do a few jobs round the cottage, mend the wall and suchlike. Don't worry. I'll be careful. And dumb."

He stands straighter these days, less stooped, and seems taller than ever, too large for the rags I have provided. He looks down at me and asks, "Are ye wondering if ye've mended a monster, mistress?"

I was.

Outside, tree branches tap at the empty window, stick against stick in the rising breeze. We both speak at the same time.

"I'm sorry... you first..."

"No... it wasnae anything..."

"I was just going to say that you're better off without your weapons, Robert. They would be incriminating. I'll give you a knife and bow to travel north with, so that you can feed yourself. What were you going to say?"

"Just... it's a pity there's warfare between our people."

"Yes."

"I'll not be coming here again. I suppose ye wouldnae..."

"What?"

"Nothing."

"You might come here again. You might raid us again if..." I break off sharply. I nearly became more of a traitor than I am already, by mentioning the raid planned by our own men against the Scottish borders. "I must go. Verity and I are taking the shearings to Kendal Wool Market today. I'll be back in a day or two."

"Come back tomorrow."

"I'll see." I kiss him on the cheek, surprising both of us. It is an apology, I tell myself, for having misled him about the weapons.

Chapter 13

I ride to Kendal on Saint Hilda, with Verity on Meadowsweet, and George and Jonah, two of Father's henchmen, on the cart with the wool. Half our shearings we keep and the other half goes to the Kendal Wool Market. The half we keep is made into woollen cloth by women from the valley, and half of that is then sold by Mother to wool merchants who travel from the south, going in a great loop from us round the wool farmers of the Yorkshire Ryddings, then down through Suffolk.

Verity is oddly quiet on the journey, but at the wool market she brightens up and bargains even better prices than usual. There is something about her which seems to say take it or leave it, I hardly care. She laughs and jokes, ignores aggression and innuendo as though they had not happened, closes deals sharply as bewildered buyers name prices they had not intended. It is all rather impressive. On the way back I ask her, "What is it, Verity? You're in a strange mood." She looks at me, her cheeks flushed but her manner edgy, and for a moment I think she is going to tell me something momentous. Then she just laughs and shrugs her shoulders.

I visit Robert the following day. I have been taking him juniper infusions to cleanse his blood, but today he pushes the cup away and says, "Enough! It's vile." He looks in dismay at the new set of clothes I have brought him. They are old and worn, filched from the cupboard at the back of the men's common room, but at least they are bigger and likely to be a better fit. He takes them away to a place upstream where the beck flows between high, mossy banks, to lie and soak himself before putting them on. When he comes back, with the clothes disdainfully half laced and flapping, he says, "Beatrice, I need to get the strength back into my arm now. Will you bring me a bow?"

I hesitate. A Scot with a weapon, on the loose in the woods, doesn't seem like a good idea.

"I could teach you to shoot, too," he adds. I stare at him. To be taught to shoot by a Scot seems the ultimate crossing of boundaries.

"I can shoot perfectly well already, thank you Robert," I reply.

"You could shoot better."

"You haven't seen me shoot."

"I don't need to. I've seen you push people off towers. That's enough. You hesitate. You fumble. I owe my life to it."

"Are you sure you want to teach me to have a more decisive attitude towards killing, then?"

"Aye, we might eat better if you go off into the forest and kill a stag or two, my sweeting. I can't yet, wi' this arm."

"Heavens above, you're criticising the service now, are you?"

We both start laughing. He takes hold of my right arm. "Are ye right-fisted?" He raises my elbow until it is level with my ear, and then slowly pulls it back. I can almost feel the arrow between my fingers, the bowstring pulling hard. Robert moves round to stand behind me, leans close, raises my left arm straight ahead of me. He says, "Bring a bow. Let me teach you."

I rub my arms. I am covered in gooseflesh. "I'll see. I'll bring you more meat anyway, Robert, some venison if I can, but I'm not going out shooting stags myself."

For the next two days I do not go to the cottage. Instead I accompany some of our henchmen who are helping the homesteaders rebuild their dwellings. There is a soothing satisfaction in seeing the open framework of upright and horizontal timber beams grow, and the vertical slats being slotted in neatly at top and bottom. I collect hazel reeds from the woods, and help weave them in.

Verity and James are helping too. His rambling stone farmhouse survived untouched, so he is helping others rebuild. The two of them work together unspeaking, chopping straw and mashing it with clay from the foreshore to daub on the woven reed walls. When it is dry the Cockleshell Man scores it with his sharp knives. He is coming in from his clifftop more often these days.

Several times I ride over the hill with the cart behind Saint Hilda to bring lime from the kiln on the other side of Hagditch. We pound it with stones until it is dust, and use it to make plaster for the outer walls. Each time I take the main track through the woods I am aware of Robert a mile to the east of me. I find that helping rebuild the houses has renewed my anger at him. I cannot bear the thought that all our hard work might be burnt down again next spring. Nevertheless, when I do return to the cottage on the third day, I take my bow with me. He wants me to be a better shot. Well, he may regret it if he should ever return.

He is up a tree. I cannot find him at first. I have come silently through the woods and he has not heard me. I find him sitting high in a beech tree, chipping away at the bark. I am able to stand for several minutes watching him before he is aware of my presence. I load an arrow and draw back the bowstring. He sees me just before I let fly. The arrow thuds into the tree trunk below him. After an initial start, he recovers his composure and laughs.

"You'll be hard put to hit a barn wi' that stance, Beatrice. Here, let me show you." He swings down from the tree. I can see that it hurts his arm, but he merely grunts. I look up to see what he has been doing in the

116

tree, then pretend I have not seen, because it is my own name carved there.

"I thought you'd abandoned me," he says.

I tell him about my work rebuilding the houses, stressing the effort involved. He does not comment, and instead starts arranging me and my bow in what seems an overly dramatic pose. I want to say to him, stop, this is ridiculous. Yet there's something about it which reminds me of the way I ministered to his limbs when he was ill, shifting them about, arranging them to my convenience. Now he arranges mine. He presses his hand to the top of my spine, saying, "Straighten your back there. Chin down. Eyes level. Look along the line of your arm. Let your arm be an extension of your eye." For a moment I think he has kissed the side of my neck, then I am not sure, and to make a fuss about it if he hadn't would make me look foolish.

Robert tries the bow himself, but his own arm is still hopelessly too weak, so he carries on teaching me through the long afternoon. He shows me how to stand. "Balance, Beatrice. Put your weight on your back foot and pivot from there. Follow your target with your eye and your hips. Have you seen statues of Diana the Huntress?"

"Nay sir, but it sounds mightily heathen." I make myself sound severe and old-fashioned, like Kate or old Parson Pattinson, and he laughs, and pretends to be afraid of me.

As twilight draws in he sets targets for me: a red leaf from autumn which has somehow escaped winter's deliquescence, a tuft of sheep's wool, a curl of bark, satiny inside. I hit most, and miss a few. His praise is disproportionate to my achievements. He says, "We'll try a moving target tomorrow. Let's you and I go hunting, Beatrice."

"Hunt with a Scot?" I laugh. "I think not, sir."

"But will you come tomorrow?"

I nod. "We shall get caught. I fear it. You must recover now, Robert, and be on your way. If I don't come back tomorrow... if it is too difficult... I've brought you enough food to last. It's nearly Midsummer. There's a lot to do. We have the Midsummer Revels in a week."

"Midsummer? Is it June already?" His eyes become distant and look past me. "I had not thought to be so far from home at Midsummer."

I gaze at him. He is a very different sight from the poor, wounded thing he was. His eyes meet mine, and for a moment we just look at one another. With his new, blooming, healthy look it is going to be harder to pretend he is a dumb vagrant, if he should be discovered. His russet hair and bright hazel eyes make him look exactly what he is, a Scot. Yet he isn't fit to go. His strength lasts no time at all. To journey to Scotland he needs to be strong enough to ride or walk for miles, hide from pursuers, forage for his own food. If only his arm were stronger I could find him a boat and he could row, but there is no likelihood of his muscles and sinews recovering enough in time for such strenuous usage. He must go, and it should be soon, but to misjudge, and for him to leave while he is still too weak, would almost certainly mean he would be caught.

He takes hold of my hand, and this time there is no mistake, when he kisses me lightly on the cheek.

On Midsummer morning I stand in the yeasty-scented dimness of the cow byre, and confront the fact that a day without visiting Robert is a day without purpose. I lean my forehead against the cool wall and think about him.

Today we are garlanding cattle for the Midsummer Bonfires. I go to where our best cow, Elizabeth, stands. She stares at me from between her long, straight lashes. Her grainy black nose gives off dampness, and small hairs stand out around it like a halo. I reach for her garland of scabious and wild roses, wound on to three thin willow branches twisted into a circle. In the rancid, fermented darkness the flowers are sweet and bright. I pull her ears through and she tries to push me away. Grassy heat from her flanks laps at me. The overblown fertility of summer is all around, and I am here, alone in it. I want company, someone to be human and ordinary amid all this rampant nature. Mother is out with the other married women of the valley, ceremonially dressing wells with flowers, to ensure us water throughout the summer. Verity is on an unexplained errand. She often is, these days. Leo and Dickon are herding the rest of the cattle into the barmkin, to stop them panicking when the bonfires are lit and the music and dancing start. Hugh... no, Hugh would not do.

I stroke Elizabeth's ridged forehead. The cattle-smelling warmth is suddenly suffocating. I get out and walk quickly up the hill, before I can start dwelling on the thought of Robert in a cowshed.

Chapter 14

People are gathering in the meadow already. Somewhere in the tower Germaine is tuning her fiddle. I hurry up the spiral staircase. In the doorway between the living hall and his room I find Father putting on his stomacher. His scented leather cloak hangs over the back of his oak chair. "Good morrow, Daughter," he greets me. He likes fairs and fests, with their reason to dress up and their excuse for getting drunk. "Are you ready to celebrate Midsummer, child?"

"Yes Father. Here, let me help you with that."

He releases the laces on his stomacher and they whip out through the holes with surprising force. The garment sags round his thighs. I start to lace him back into it and he says, "Your Uncle Juniper and I are concerned, Beatrice."

"Oh?" I look up at him.

"You and your sister are reputed to be running wild. Your uncle wishes to set a date for the betrothals."

"And you, Father?" I observe the shake in his hands as I lace the last of the holes and tie a firm double bow.

"Aye well." He looks at me for a moment, then says, "We have to have grandchildren for the farms, Beatie, you know that. You can't put it off for ever."

I straighten up. "Give me until winter, Father." The Cockleshell Man's words are in my head: he'll be fit to move by Allhallows, and home before winter sets in. I just need until winter. I drape my father's cloak round his shoulders. "Father, how would it be if Verity and I stopped running wild and you stayed off the highways?"

I have misjudged. I know it at once. Father's brows draw together and his cheeks turn mottled. I back away, and am gone before he can co-ordinate his limbs to follow me, but I have wondered many times since, if I had not angered him then, if he had not been angry to start with, whether things might have been different later.

Bonfires have been lit at the four corners of the long lea on the sea side of our tower. Homesteaders from all along the valley have brought their best cows or goats with garlands round their necks. The animals are all tethered round the meadow, and have set up a great commotion, disliking the smoke and excitement in the air. Their bellowing adds a sense of wildness to the celebrations.

I put on a red silk skirt and chemise which Mother made for me from the material which Gerald bought Verity at the

May Fair, and which she threw out of the window when she arrived home. Over it I lace an embroidered cream bodice. Then I stick a rose in my hair and go out to play.

"Oh Lordy me, she looks like a gypsy," Kate mutters as I pass her in the gatehouse. I notice that she is also uncharacteristically bedecked and frilled.

Simon Sims, a travelling pedlar minstrel who visits us every year at Midsummer, has arrived with his fiddle, so we are spared Germaine's playing. She comes over to join me, looking spectacular in grass-green silk. It's Midsummer; I'm feeling good. I smile and walk down the hill with her, and into the crowd to dance.

The dancing is in its first frenzy on the straw-strewn grass. We make up formations without thought, and whirl around, partnering anyone who happens to be near. After a while, out of breath, we stop, and gather round the minstrel to hear the latest gossip from across the north of England. He brings news of more devastation wrought by the Scots. "Fifteen died at Nether Kellet," he intones. We knew this already, but he has a dramatic way of telling it. "Pillage and plunder at Priest Hutton. Twenty stone houses burnt to the ground at Keswick. All t'crops of oats and barley burnt at Allithwaite..."

We cluck our tongues and lean closer to hear how much worse others have fared than we have.

"They came by sea, here," Kate offers, for we have to replenish his store of gossip, by way of payment. "They took all the cattle from over at Mere Point."

"Aye?" Simon shakes his head. "It were horseback riders further north. Regular moss-troopers. I reckon your boat-pirates'd pass t'cattle on to them." He laughs, showing big, strong teeth. "They'd hardly tek 'em back by boat, would they!"

After further exchange of horrors he takes up his fiddle again and starts playing *Shepherd's Hey*. Hugh arrives on his new horse, a tall roan gelding which has replaced his stolen one. He tethers it at the beck and comes to find me, and we dance together. The music is growing wilder, the cattle lowing more loudly. Suddenly amid the din there is the unmistakeable sound of a goatskin drum, picking up the rhythm of Simon's fiddle. It is James Sorrell, sitting on one of the hay bales at the edge of the dance. I know he has been making this drum for weeks. Now the heel of his hand comes down on the tooled leather in beautiful, perfect time. I dance past him and wave, and he flings his hand into the air in greeting without missing a beat.

Gerald and Germaine appear to have gone mad. They are clasped together, swaying to the beat of the music. I wonder whether to go and warn them that Father is coming out, but what happens next makes the thought irrelevant. Verity has appeared next to James. She stands with her hand on his shoulder, smiling down at him. He beats out a fast drumroll with the flats of his hands, then stands up and kisses her. There are some ways in which James's timing is not of the best.

People near them stop dancing and stare. Verity pulls free, not horrified but amused. The next moment a violent blow sends James lurching to his knees, and my father stands over him, crimson-faced and gasping.

"Get away from my daughter, lout!" he shrieks. The music dies. A murmur runs round the crowd. My father raises his handpecke, the small axe with one flat end and one pointed, with which he beheads chickens. For a moment it seems he will bring it down on James's head. Instead he swings it high and smashes it into the drum. The decorated leather bursts open.

"Father!" Verity's rage is shocking because it is real, not the usual rough teasing with which she and Father address each other. She snatches the axe away from him. "How *dare* you!"

There is a moment of teetering violence between them. They stare into each other's eyes. Behind them, James gets slowly to his feet, a look of fury on his face. I can see that Father is bemused. He had thought he was rescuing Verity. He says, "Daughter...?"

Verity takes James's hand. She says, "I should like to marry James Sorrell, if I may have your permission, Father." Her voice is shaking. Absolute silence falls across the crowd.

It looks for a moment as if Father is going to suffer an apoplexy. His cheeks darken to purple. His nose stands out, almost blue. He is incapable of speech. Then, slowly, he begins to laugh. He says, "I like your wit, Daughter," and sets off back up the hill to the tower, muttering, "Very good. Oh, very good."

Verity stares after him. Her chin is trembling. She shouts, "I will never marry Gerald! Do you hear me, Father? Never never never!" She is in tears. I put my arms round her but she pushes me away. "Where were you when I needed you, Beatrice? Off in the forest with Hugh? You're on their side, not mine!" I stare at her in shock.

People are hesitating, some turning away, not wishing to get on the wrong side of Father. Leo hands James his drum and mutters, "It'll mend, lad." Hugh gestures to Simon Sims to start playing again. Germaine, well away from Gerald now, finds her fiddle and joins him. They play together, dancing round each other, grinning, colliding elbows and hips in fun, making people laugh. Gradually the mood of festivity is restored.

Verity says to me, "I'm sorry, Sister," and she and James walk away together towards the Pike, with a cold dignity that rejects us all. She is sobbing. A little way down the slope James puts his arm round her. I watch them go. Hugh holds out his hand to me, but I shake my head. There is only one place I want to be at the moment, and it is not here.

I ride Saint Hilda through the woods at a fast trot. Half way to the cottage I meet Mother, strolling from the direction of the shore with an unhurried smile on her face and fish scales in her hair. She looks surprised to see me.

"Beatie, where are you off to? I thought you'd be dancing till midnight."

I jump off Saint Hilda and hug her. "I need to get away for a bit, Mother. Are you going home? Father and Verity have quarrelled. She may need to talk to you when she comes down from the Pike."

Mother looks dismayed. "I'd better get on home then." She bites her lip. "I shouldn't be away so much. Go on. Enjoy your ride."

I put one foot in the stirrup. I feel a great urgency to talk to her properly, and for us not to have secrets. Secrets have led to Verity's accusation that I have neglected her, that I am not on her side. Robert is a secret which I cannot share, but he makes all other secrets seem unworthy of the bother of keeping them. Yet how can I ask my mother if the local witchdoctor is her lover?

"Mother..."

"Yes child?" She sounds impatient. I reach into my saddlebag where I have a leather pouch belonging to the Cockleshell Man. It contained painkilling herbs when Robert still needed them. I have been meaning to return it to him.

"Would you mind giving this back to Cedric, please?"

Her mouth actually falls open, and stays so. Her round blue eyes just gawp at me. The colour goes from her face.

I am alarmed. "I'm sorry, Mother. I shouldn't have said anything."

She passes a shaking hand over her face. "Is this your way of questioning me, Beatrice?"

I realise then that I do not need to question her. My mother loves the Cockleshell Man. It is perfectly obvious, and indeed I do not blame her. I shake my head. "No Mother. No, it isn't."

"How do you know him, Beatrice? What was in this pouch?"

"A... remedy... some herbs for someone I know..."

"I'm surprised you didn't mention it to me then, and that Cedric didn't say he had met you."

This is a talent my mother has, gently changing the emphasis and putting the other person on the defensive. I feel very close to her suddenly. She and I are both doing the unthinkable. I kiss her on the cheek, and realise with relief that if Cedric has not told her about meeting me, he will certainly not have mentioned Robert to anyone else. My mother says, "He is a man of exceptional goodness, Beatrice. You will know that if you have met him." She takes the pouch from me and nods, then walks away quickly through the forest.

Chapter 15

Robert is not at the cottage. He is not anywhere I look. I search the woods. I even risk calling him. Some half-fletched arrows he has whittled lie outside the cottage. The grey goose feathers he has been using to fletch them are blowing about in the breeze. I look for a note, then realise I don't even know if he can read and write.

Has he gone? Has he just decided he is well enough, and returned to Scotland? He sounded very homesick yesterday. I shiver, despite the heat. Surely he will not have tried to cross the sands unaided. Our quicksands are shifting, treacherous things, and all travellers must be guided across. Cedric is the guide, or carter, as we call him. I did not see him at the Midsummer Revels, so perhaps he is at this moment taking Robert across the sands, or perhaps he took him last night, in the safety of darkness.

I feel astonished that Robert should have left without saying goodbye to me. I ought to feel relieved, but I do not, though I can see the sense in his going now, before our march on Scotland draws closer and the communal blood is up.

I search the woods one more time, then untether Saint Hilda from beside the beck. The sun is tilting towards the west on this longest day of summer. It is going to be a golden evening. The tide is moving up the bay as I ride back down the hill towards the lea. The midsummer bonfires are now emitting just a heat haze. Germaine in her green silk gown is sitting on a logpile, playing a lament on her fiddle. A drunken farmhand lurches out of the bushes at me, his face red and his clothing dishevelled. "I'm ready to fight the bloody Scots," he declares, and falls into a patch of thistles.

I continue down towards the tower. Torches have been lit along the valley to see merrymakers home, and the hot smell of tar mingles with the smell of dung. A few homesteaders are still standing around, talking and laughing. Dickon is dancing to the tune Germaine is playing, a pair of ram's horns held to his head. Around us, twilight deepens. It gradually occurs to me that something is wrong. There is a strange atmosphere, a sense of suppressed excitement amongst those who remain. I hand Saint Hilda over to Leo, and almost ask him what is going on, but do not wish to draw attention to the fact that I have been absent.

In the kitchen Kate is suspending a pot from the top notch of the rackencrock, for a slow stewing. Clearly supper is expected to be late. "Kate, what's happening?" I ask. "It feels as if something is going on."

She turns the handle of the winch which swings the rackencrock back over the flames, and throws me a disapproving, purse-lipped look. "Those of us not dallying out in t'woods know as to what's going on, my girl."

I turn away impatiently, but Kate, unwilling to let anyone else be the bearer of scandalous tidings, adds smoothly, "'Tis a death hunt."

I freeze. Suddenly the smoke from the midsummer bonfires has a sickening odour. "Who is it? Who are they hunting this time?" I ask.

Kate, her face red from the fire, allows a dramatic pause before she whispers, "They found a Scot in the woods."

I feel as if I am going to pass out. Kate wipes her hands, bloodstained from cutting up the mutton, on the white apron which now covers her frilled gown. I lower myself on to the oak settle. "You say a death hunt, Kate? So he must have got away then."

"Aye, the lads were too drunk to hold him. He'll not get far though. They'll comb t'district and cut off the route round the bay. If he tries to cross the sands, well God help him. It'll save us a bit of bother."

A large, white moth flutters past me into the fire, and fizzes audibly to death. Despite the heat, gooseflesh is

131

standing out along my arms and legs, living flesh which will also be consigned to the fire if I am caught in what I am about to do. I stand up. "Kate, I'm going to bed. Death hunts sicken me. Don't disturb me for supper."

Kate weighs her cleaver in her hands. "Oh, hoity toity then. That makes two of you. Mistress Verity is sickly and lying down too."

I leave while she is still talking, then put my head back round the kitchen arch. "Kate, where did they find him, this Scot?"

"In the ash grove by the lime quarry, is what I heard. Meks yer blood run cold."

The ash grove – he'll have been cutting sticks for the arrows he's making. How could he be so stupid as to come out into the open like that? I feel furious with him, after all the care we have taken. I run up the stairs to my room. The stairwell is full of acrid pitch smoke which has drifted in through the arrow slits. I arrive in my room coughing. At my window I can hear the voices of people outside in the barmkin. More seem to be arriving and everyone sounds drunk. Tinderboxes click and spark. Through the distorting glass I can see glimmers of flame as torches flare up. I go up on to the battlements, where Martinus and George are watching the crowd below.

"They reckon as he's an outrider for a fresh attack," George tells me. "Unless he was left behind from last time."

A cheer goes up below. I peer over and see my father wobbling drunkenly on the barmkin wall, calling to his horse, Caligula. Someone brings the horse over and he topples on to it. The barmkin gate swings open and the assembly bunches together. The few horses prance and fidget. A howl arises from the edge of the darkening woods. Master Spearing, who keeps the alehouse in the village of Barrowbeck, has arrived with his two manhunting bratch-hounds. I watch them being offered a bundle of some sort, and then recognise the red-brown jerkin I gave Robert from the cupboard at the back of the men's common room. I realise not only that its previous owner could easily recognise it, but that my scent as well as Robert's might be on it.

Slowly the death hunt moves off, the walkers keeping clear of the nervous frisking of the horses. I bid the two henchmen good night and walk to the top of the stairs, then as soon as I am out of sight, run for my room. Caesar, my cat, races with me, enjoying the game. I push him away, fling my hooded black cloak round my shoulders and flee down the back stairs.

I pass the end of the bright kitchen without Kate seeing me, then rush on down the underground passage, past the wolf-pit, up through the stone floor of the dairy and out into the barmkin. Saint Hilda approaches, but I stroke her warm neck and leave her behind. I need to be inconspicuous. Out in the cool meadow, wisps of smoke hover about my shoulders and a pale, daylight moon shines on the sea at the end of the valley. Robert, what are you feeling, out there in the dark? I don't think you're easily afraid, but perhaps you're afraid now. Can you hear the dogs?

The hunters on horseback are keeping a close rein, letting the hounds take their time and allowing those walking to keep up. I move silently behind them. It is not difficult to be unheard, with the noise of the dogs' yelping and whining. At the crossroads on the Barrowbeck to Hagditch Road the death hunt stops, and flounders about uncertainly. I press myself against the trunk of a tree. "The hounds are favouring that way." Someone points.

"Aye, reckon as he's headed for Mistholme Moss." It is my father's voice.

Suddenly I know where Robert is. Yesterday I told him the truth about his weapons. They are indeed at the bottom of a bog, but what I had omitted to tell him before was that they are wrapped in oilcloth and attached to a long, fine chain, so that they can be hauled back to the surface when necessary. I suppose it was a dislike of waste that made me do it. They are fine, well-tooled weapons. A lot of work went into them.

The death hunt moves off in the opposite direction from Barrowbeck, towards Mistholme Moss. I know this marsh well. It is where we cut peat and gather rushes. There is a short cut to it over a gorse-scattered heath full of rough stones and lacerating thorns, on the opposite side of the road from where I stand. If I go that way, I can reach Mistholme Moss ahead of the death hunt. I hitch up my skirts, climb the steep bank and start fighting my way through the hostile scrubland.

I wonder if Robert will have found, in the wilderness of pools and reedbeds that is Mistholme Moss, the ancient stand of willows which I described to him. By day it would be easy. "Where the yellow flags are in bloom," I told him. Whether he will be able to make out these wild irises in the dark is another matter. The intermittent bright moonlight will be both his ally and his enemy.

For a long time, as I stumble across the heath, I can see the torches of the death hunt as they take the easier route. My own way is frighteningly slow. Spiny shrubs catch on my skirts and drag me back. In places the gorse and bracken are impenetrable, and I have to make detours over high escarpments and low fissures. My stockings become ripped and full of thorns. At last I climb down the bank to the Mistholme Road and stand still, to listen. The death hunt must be far behind me now. There is a chance.

Water glimmers ahead, dappled bright and dull in patches where pool and reedbed intermingle, like a tapestry of silk and wool. An owl hoots from the hill over which I have come, and another replies from the wooded rise across the moss. I pick my way down the pebbled slope to where the ground is soft, and risk calling, "Robert?" There is no reply. Water seeps round my boots as I edge carefully on to a safe path and make my way towards the willows.

I am walking between sheets of water now, their surface puckered by a breeze which sends long, flat ripples smacking at the path edge. Somewhere near me a duck mutters in its sleep. Small clumps of water-weed look like warts on skin. As I near the willows a splash sounds ahead of me, but it is only a sleepless otter. I call again, "Robert?"

I try to work out where the death hunt will be now. They can't be far behind. Ahead of me the thick-knit stand of willows blots out the moon. Slippery things move beneath my feet. Small bodies slap into the water as frogs flee my path, and I only realise when the silence intensifies, that their trilling had filled the air before.

Robert is not among the willows. I go to the low-hanging branch where I attached the other end of the chain holding his weapons, and feel along it. I tread over my boots in water as I check again. The weapons have gone.

Then I hear them. The death hunt has reached the moss. The dogs sound excited, as if they have picked up a trail. Is it Robert's, or mine, I wonder. I stand still, trying to work out which path they will take. I am going to have to make a wide detour now, on paths I know less well. I climb through the willows and feel around with my foot for where the path continues, but I cannot find it. There seems to be just a sheet of water here. I climb back and take an unreliable, boggy path which will come out a long way back down the Mistholme Road. Where I come out is the least of my worries now.

Suddenly the dogs are baying. Dear God, they must have scented me. They must know that I held that jerkin, carried it through the woods, helped Robert get his bad arm in and out of it. I try to walk faster, and immediately fall into the bog. Cold, peaty water closes over my head. I choke, surface, clamber out again, my wet cloak half strangling me. I want to empty the water from my boots, but daren't stop. Somewhere, very close, something growls. The moon has gone behind a cloud. I stand still and wait to be attacked, then realise it was the water gurgling back through the reeds that border the path.

Far off to my left I can hear men shouting. The dogs are setting up a new clamour. The water seems to carry the sound within it. My teeth start chattering and my whole body shakes with cold and fright. Is Robert over there? Have they caught him? Suddenly the moon comes out, and I can see the road. I stagger towards it and drag myself up the pebbled shore. I just want to lie there, on dry earth, but there is no time. I can see a halo of light far off down the road, where torchlight reflects off rocks. I start to run towards it, then climb up the rocks to look down on the road. The death hunt is milling about below me. Someone is refreshing the scent of the dogs. So they haven't caught him yet. There is someone else there too, and voices raised in anger. I edge forward, my wet boots squeaking and slipping on the rocks. It is Parson Becker on his black horse, and he and my father are shouting at each other. Master Spearing's bratch-hounds start snapping at John Becker's horse's heels, but the animal does not move. I know he calls his horse Universe. As though encouraged by the dogs, several men move menacingly towards the priest. I am just above him. I can hear him sigh in exasperation.

"This is not the way to do it." He raises himself slightly in the stirrups, leaning his hands on the pommel of the saddle. "Look, you've lost his scent. You'll never find it again amongst all this water. Why do you think he came this way? *If* he exists at all. If you all stayed sober you'd be in a better state to know whether you're seeing Scotsmen or not. Try to cross that bog now and a couple of you will drown before the night's out. Go home instead, and pray for better sense." Suddenly he brings his whip down sharply across his gloved hand. "Squire Garth, go *home*, then the others will follow you."

I watch the wind ruffle John Becker's hair as he sits back down. My father shifts in his own saddle, then abruptly wheels his horse and raps away smartly through the middle of the crowd, shouting over his shoulder, "We'll catch him in the morning! Yon prating parson'll be eating his words then." The crowd scatters in panic from my father's horse, then gradually starts to disperse.

I wait until the road is empty, except for the priest on his horse, then I climb down the rocks. John looks shocked.

"Beatrice. I didn't expect to see you on a death hunt."

"I wasn't on the hunt."

He looks at me more closely. "You're soaking wet. Whatever's happened?"

I want to tell him the whole story, but the risk is too

great. He is staring at me curiously. After a moment he holds down his hand to me. "Climb up. I'll take you home."

I come close against the warmth of his horse's side and his booted leg. "No thank you, John. I have something else to do."

He dismounts. "Beatrice, I hardly dare think what you're up to." He touches my dripping hair. "At least swap cloaks then." He pulls my drenched cloak off my shoulders, and flings his own round me. It smells of him, and feels warm and dry over the sodden red silk, which it seems I put on such a long time ago.

"Thank you." I turn away, before I can be tempted to give in and ride home with him. I cross the Barrowbeck road and climb the steep bank to the woods. When I glance back he is on his horse at the crossroads, looking first along the Mistholme road which borders the bog, and then along the Barrowbeck to Hagditch road which borders the woods. It is as if he were looking for someone.

As I step over the bracken to find the path amongst the trees he walks his horse over to the bottom of the steep bank and calls up to me, "Be careful, Beatrice."

"Yes." I look down at him, then plunge into the leafy darkness.

The forest is more dangerous at night. I keep to the paths, no matter how small, for fear of snares set by trappers. I move slowly, in order to be silent, knowing I am good at being silent, thankful when the moon comes out from behind the clouds and makes it easier. I am not even sure that Robert will have returned to the cottage, but even if he hasn't, then I think he will be somewhere near. He will want me to find him.

It is much further, coming this way. There are places where it is completely dark. As I stop to find my bearings, I realise suddenly that I have been hearing a sound which I can't identify, a sort of hushing burr. I stand absolutely still and listen. Probably most people would not have heard it, it is so faint and far off, but I have become attuned to the forest these past months, my senses heightened and my hearing sharper than ever. All around me the normal night sounds of the greenwood continue. I move. It is there again. It moves when I move. It is behind me.

I pull my skirts close. Could it be the sound of my own movement through the brambles? No, my hitched up skirts make no sound. I hear it again. It has an animal purposefulness. It is not the wind in the branches, nor the far-off rippling of the beck. Then my flesh creeps on my bones as I realise what it is. It is air through wet jaws, a damp snuffling close to the ground amongst the leaves. It is the sound of a dog following a trail.

I want to scream and run. Instead I wait and listen. I clamp my hands to a tree branch to stop myself shaking. It is quite far back, a careful, silent animal stalking the quarry whose scent it has been given, and whom it does not wish to alarm until it is close enough to pounce. It has the scent of Robert's jerkin in its clever nose, the jerkin which I carried close against me all the way from the tower. Master Spearing's bratch-hound is stalking me.

I try to quell my terror and the urge to run for my life, and instead struggle to consider my options. I cannot outrun this beast. It is faster than I am. I cannot continue heading for the cottage either, and risk leading it to Robert. If I could just reach the beck before it sees me, I could wade downstream and it would not be able to follow my trail in the water. It would not know if I had gone upstream or downstream, and even if it were to choose correctly, it would take a long time finding where I had eventually climbed out on to the bank again.

I edge off noiselessly to my left, leaving the path, risking the snares. Small twigs crackle under my feet. I stop. The dog has stopped too. I can sense it listening. I move on, curling my toes on tree roots and rocks, trying to ease myself silently over the ground. Mist floats amongst tree trunks ahead of me, and I can hear and smell water. Terrifyingly, the sound of the beck is drowning out the noise of my pursuer. I move more quickly, hoping it is drowning out my own sounds too. Suddenly the ground drops away, and I almost fall into the deep cleft in the woods where the beck runs. Thank God! I stoop to scramble down the slope backwards on my hands and knees, and the dog rushes at me out of the darkness.

Its face is huge, its lips drawn back above dripping teeth. It raises its head and gives a high, belling cry.

Faintly, from far off, other dogs answer it. Then it runs at me, snarling, its lips quivering, its muscular shoulders high. I recoil and slither part way down the slope. It follows me, snapping at my face. I realise I know this dog. It is Mad Joly, Master Spearing's oldest bratch-hound. She comes after me, catching my sleeve with her fangs and ripping it. I scream, "Joly! Stop! Stop it, good dog! You know me!" She hesitates. Moonlight struggles through the trees and shows a corner of red silk caught on her teeth. I wonder where Master Spearing is. I try to pull myself to my feet, wobbling on the steep slope. I must not fall. She would pursue me and tear me to pieces if I did. As we stand, both indecisive, there is movement on the path above, and the excited panting of more dogs.

"Hold him, girl!" It is Master Spearing. "Well done, lass! Hold t'bastard!"

"Master Spearing!" I call hoarsely. "Master Spearing, please call your dog off."

His face looms above me, his mouth agawp. For a moment he is speechless, then he takes Mad Joly by the scruff of her neck and pulls her away. "Daft bugger, yon's Mistress Garth. Oh Lordy me, sorry lady. Joly's getting past it." He reaches down to help me. I let him haul me up the bank. I find that I am shaking and unable to speak. "I'm right sorry about t'dog, mistress. Were you on t'death hunt? You're tekking a long way home, aren't you?"

I nod again, and manage to stutter, "It's owls, you see, Master Spearing. I'm studying owls. My teacher, Master

Becker..." I'm babbling now. "Master Becker... he sets us tasks for our studies... and this month it's owls..."

Master Spearing stares at me, then shakes his head. "Owls? Well I never. What does he want to teach you little ladies about owls for? It's not as if you could cook 'em..."

After I have refused Master Spearing's offers to see me home, and listened to his warnings about mad bogeymen Scots loose in the woods, I wait until he has been gone a comfortable time, then tackle the task of finding the cottage from this direction. Eventually I see its hunched, bramble-covered shape as an irregularity in the pattern of the forest. I sidle from tree to tree. The moon has gone behind a cloud again, but I can see that the door is open. I mould myself to the doorframe and peer in. Two red eyes look back at me.

All the hairs along the back of my neck stand up. For a moment I think Mad Joly has followed me, then I realise it is a fox which has moved in and is finishing off Robert's food, a young vixen, still with a fluffiness in her russet coat. I call to her softly. She stands with the leftover bread and cheese clamped in her mouth, strings of saliva dribbling to the ground. I step back to let her out, but she in her turn is waiting for me to go. It is obvious that Robert is not here. I take another step back, to leave her in peace, and an arm seizes me from behind. From the other side a hand clamps over my mouth. My head is dragged back against someone's body. I can't move or speak.

I struggle, and try to scream. The fox patters out past me. Robert's voice says, "Shhh. There now. Sorry Beatrice. Sorry." He lets go, and I almost fall into the cottage.

"Dear Lord, Robert, have you not heard of announcing yourself?" I collapse on to the floor. The smell of fox is very strong.

He kneels next to me, facing the door, a dagger in his hand. He whispers, "The deer hunters are about. Stay quiet. They may not have heard us. I couldn't risk you speaking when you saw me. You're a quiet one, Beatrice. Yon vixen makes more noise than you do. What's happened to your clothes? Are you all right? "

I nod, finding I am more than all right. "I met the dogs going home. They had my scent as well as yours, but it was all right."

"Mother of God! Are you sure you're all right?"

I burst into tears and put my arms round him. "Are *you* all right?" I realise then that he is as wet as I am, and shivering with cold and weakness. I remember how all this started, and suddenly I am angry. "How could you be so stupid?" I demand. "For the sake of a few sticks for arrows, Robert? Truly, that fox has more sense than you do."

He holds me a little back from him, and flicks the dagger so that it lands quivering in the ground. "I needed arrows, darling, and I needed my weapons back. I couldn't ask you." Then he holds my soggy body against his, kneeling there, and presses his face into my neck.

My tears drip into his hair. "You're going then? You're going now?"

"I have to. Where can I find Cedric, to see me over the sands? I wish my arm were strong enough to row, then I could take a boat and go at high tide, but it's still too weak. It would let me down. I'll have to cross the sands and walk across the mountains, unless the monks can give me a fast horse to take my chances on."

"They're very poor. It's unlikely they'll have horses. Anyway you'll be safer on foot. It will be easier to hide, and make your way gradually through the mountains. I'll see Cedric, but you must rest overnight. Look at you." I hold up his arm. It is trembling.

He pulls it away and says, "Beatrice, come with me."

I am not surprised. The unasked question has hung in the air between us for weeks. It is a shock to hear it finally spoken, though. I look into his face. Even in the darkness it has become, once again, the face at the window. I shake my head. "It's impossible."

"Scotland is beautiful, Beatrice. Plenty of English girls have crossed the border. You must know what I'm feeling about you." When I don't reply he adds, "We get on well enough, don't we? Tell me truthfully what you feel." He grips my arms.

I pull free of him and stand up. "Robert, I couldn't leave my family. They need me. I have to stay and marry my cousin."

"Oh yes, Hughie. Good little Hughie whom you don't

145

love." Robert also stands up. "Beatrice you have nothing but trouble from your family. You'd like my family, my mother, father and brothers. I live in a pele tower like yours. Please consider it..."

I shake my head. "It's impossible, Robert. You must see. I could never do it, betray my people, go over to the enemy."

He puts his arms round me again and kisses my forehead. "Then I shan't go. I shall stay until you change your mind."

"Robert, for heaven's sake, don't be ridiculous. They're *looking* for you."

"I shall stay until harvest. You can visit me here or not, as you please. I'm quite capable of looking after myself now. I shall get my strength back, and then at harvest I shall go. Think about it, Beatrice. Think about coming with me. As for them looking for me, well, I can deal with that." He is stripping his wet clothes off.

I ask, "Where did you hide from the death hunt?"

"Under water, by the willows. I kept my nose out, amongst the tree roots, at the far side. You nearly trod on me."

I stare at him. "Dear God. *That* was why the water was over the path."

"I watched you fall in yourself. I thought I'd have to come and save you, but you didnae give me the opportunity."

"Why didn't you speak, let me know you were safe?"

"It would have put us both in more danger. I'd have

had to come out. You'd never have seen me in the dark. We'd have made sounds, ripples. The dogs were too close to risk it. It was best for you to get as far away from me as possible." He finds the old clothes of my father's which were too short for him, in a corner, and pulls them on over his damp limbs, then hands me the wet ones. "Beatrice. Bea. What does Hughie call you?"

"Beatie."

"Bea then, will you take these and leave them out on the shore? I'll steal a horse and give it its freedom on the moors. One way or another, they'll be fairly sure I've gone."

I look at him in the darkness. An owl hoots overhead. In the distance foxes call. Robert is like a fox, the fox the raider, the fox the bright and beautiful force of nature. I roll the wet clothes into a bundle. "Robert, you stay hidden. I'll see to the horse. We have a young one, barely broken, who would dearly like to be back in the wild." I put down the wet bundle and take hold of his face between my hands. "If you're set on staying, I can't stop you, and I cannot deny that it makes me very glad, but you would be safer to go. Even as weak as you are, you would be safer to go. Cedric is always out on the sands at early low tide, collecting cockles. If I don't find you here tomorrow, I shall know you've seen sense and gone." I kiss him on the cheek, wrap my cloak round me and leave. Saying goodbye is impossible.

Chapter 16

I arrive home from leaving the wet clothes on the shore just before dawn, when the tops of the trees on Beacon Hill are starting to show like lace against the sky. This is no time to be stealing a horse. The sheep have begun bleating down on the shoreline, seagulls are calling over the bay and the owls have hushed into silence. I climb the barmkin wall on the far side rather than open the gate with its big, clanking latch, then when I can see the henchman on the battlements moving out of sight, I quickly open the gate from the inside, and lead Rosalind, our wild new filly, out by the mane. She wheels and tries to kick me, then to bite me. Frankly I shall be glad to see the back of her. One-handed, I push the gate to, but leave it unlatched, knowing that none of the other horses will stray, then I walk Rosalind a little way down the valley before swinging up to ride awkwardly astride her – how on earth men manage to ride like this all the time is a mystery to me – and head for the hills.

It is daylight when I creep exhaustedly home. Those I meet assume I have risen early, and I do my best to preserve an appearance of virtuous and well-rested diligence. I keep John Becker's cloak tightly round me, to disguise the fact that I am still in yesterday's clothes. Then I go to my room, tear off the red silk which has dried stiffly on me, and fall asleep almost before I have climbed into bed. This is how I miss what happens.

Faintly, in my sleep, I hear shouting, and I assume that Rosalind the horse has been missed, but I am too tired to wake properly. When I do finally wake, the sun is half way up the sky. No one has come to find me. They must have assumed that I am on watch, or pursuing my own tasks. I put on a loose linen shift and coarse woven bodice, and go downstairs.

On my way down I think about what I shall say to Robert, if he has not seen sense and gone. I think about how easy it is to steal a horse, and that I must do something about security. I pause by one of the arrow slits and enjoy the smell of damp earth after early morning rain. A feeling of optimism rises in me. Robert has survived the night and the death hunt. I lean my elbows on the wide inner part of the sill and gaze out through the arrow slit. Low mist hovers in the grass, and a group of men are walking down the valley looking unconnected to the ground. My father is at the head of them. I feel a first pang of disquiet.

The kitchen is empty. Now things really don't feel right. I run back upstairs to find Verity, and I can hear Kate's weeping long before I reach Verity's room.

My sister is lying on the stone floor. Her face is bleeding. Her arm looks dislocated. Kate is trying to get her to stand up. My mother is sitting on the bench by the wall, staring at nothing.

"Dear God, what...?"

Kate looks round and says, "Your father."

"What? Why?" I rush over to Verity and join Kate in trying to help her up. My sister's head lolls and she gazes blankly at me. I realise she is stunned. I turn to Mother and ask, "Have you sent for the doctor?" I feel stunned myself. I cannot think what has been the cause of this. My mother's faraway look gradually focuses on me. I assume she is even more shocked than I am, and cannot pull herself together, though that is unlike her. I stand up. "Mother, will you please send a horseman for the doctor?" I ask firmly and loudly. "I am going to help Verity to bed."

My mother says, "I have sent for Cedric."

"She's confused." Kate starts to cry again. "The mistress is befuddled by it all. She hasn't been anywhere or sent for anyone. She's just been sitting there."

I look at my mother, who for a moment is gone back again, inside her head, and I feel my spine prickle. I say to Kate, "No... I think she has sent for someone."

We help Verity to bed, and the movement seems to bring her round. Suddenly she is agitated. She seizes my arm and looks up at me. Her mouth is swollen and bleeding where a tooth has gone through her lip. A droplet of blood oozes on to tight, purple skin. She says in a hoarse voice, "Beatrice, save James. Warn him. They're going to kill him."

A cold breeze blows in, chilling me through. "Where is he?" I whisper.

"On watch on the Pike. No one else knows, because he exchanged watch with me, but they'll be hunting him. Tell him to go to the parsonage. He'll be safe there."

I nod. "All right. Yes, I will. But Verity, why on earth did Father...?"

Kate says grimly, "She and t'master quarrelled over Master James. She defied him outright." She jerks her chin in Verity's direction. "Your father said she'd not be fit to marry anyone by the time he'd finished with her."

I stare at my sister, mystified that she can want James so much. Verity groans and touches her lip, then says with difficulty, "Will you get moving, Beatie? Why? You want to know why I want to marry James? So that I can get away from this infernal household. So that I can get away from the appalling notion that I should marry Gerald. So that Low Back Farm can be mine, Beatie, all mine, and I can fill it with my children and do everything my own way." She leans back against the bolsters, tries to smile, winces at the pain. "However none of this will work

151

unless you get James away from here until Father has calmed down."

Kate clicks her tongue and crosses the room to confer with Mother. I put my arm round Verity. "But you have us here, Verity. You do things your own way here."

Her lip quivers. She speaks suddenly in the voice of a long-ago Verity, from a time when we were children. "When are you ever here, Beatie?" she asks. "Since Hugh started talking of wedding, you have never been here. I'm pleased for you that you find his company so all-absorbing, but I have been managing here on my own. Talking to myself. I might as well talk to myself on my own land."

It isn't Hugh. The words are on my lips, on the verge of being said. Wanting to be said. As if she senses it, Verity frowns at me and asks, "Is it that? Is it so wonderful with Hugh that you have no time for your family here?"

I pause, and moisten my lips, which suddenly feel very dry, and instead of answering her, I ask the selfsame question back, under my breath, because it is something I really want to know. "Is it so wonderful, Verity? With you and James?"

Beyond the pallor and the bruising a flush rises in her cheeks. She does not answer me because Mother is suddenly back with us, putting an arm around Verity and saying, "Fetch hot water and cloths please, Kate. Let's clean her up." She nods at me. "Take my horse and go and

152

get James, Beatie. She'll climb the Pike better than Saint Hilda. Take another one for James. We've had that fast new filly stolen in the night. They reckon the Scot took her and got clean away on her, so you'd better take Meadowsweet for James."

I hurry out and pass Kate on the stairs. She mutters a blessing to ward off the evil of having passed on the stairs, and adds darkly, "I reckon as t'master was right," before stamping off up the stairs. I gather up my skirts and run down to the gatehouse.

I have watched plenty of harsh physical assaults in my sixteen years of life, on both people and animals. You can't avoid it, can you, what with hunting and bear-baiting and cock-fighting and dog-fighting and slaughtering the pig for winter, not to mention attacks by Scots and disagreements between neighbours. There are burnings and hangings too, with their smells of blood and smoke and rank panic lingering long after. Violence is part of life, and one can do nothing about it. Perhaps the disgust and horror I feel is a sign of my own weakness.

I sometimes wonder about you, reader of my story, my invisible friend, separate from me in time and place. Are you gentle or brutalised? Do you watch the burnings and bear-baitings, or do you stay at home?

George and Martinus have stayed at home. I can see them on the battlements now, watching and pointing, as

I run down the hill towards the barmkin. I decide, after all, against taking the horses. Saddling up will take too long, and we would be more conspicuous on horseback. I run down the valley behind the backs of the death hunt, mostly men on foot as far as I can see at this distance. I take the middle way up the Pike, not the screes down which the Scots came, nor the usual well-trodden path we take to go on watch, but a steep, less used path which approaches the lookout post from behind. As soon as I arrive I know that something has gone badly wrong. There is no sign of James. I look round and call him. He takes his lookout duties seriously and would be unlikely to forget. I move along the summit of the Pike, to the steep drop above the screes. I can see up the valley towards Mere Point, and down the valley towards the homesteaders' dwellings, almost as far as the village of Barrowbeck itself. On this high promontory the sea is on three sides of me. Our own tower is visible on the low knoll at the far side of the valley. James's farmhouse is the first dwelling to the north-east of ours.

I climb into the lower branches of a giant yew tree which overhangs the scree, filled with an overwhelming premonition of disaster, and crane my neck. The mist is clearing now, shifting into small cloudlets in the clumps of tall grass over the cowpats. I can make out the tiny figures of Father, William and Jonah, with two new henchmen who joined us last Lady Day. They are emerging now from James's farmhouse. I wonder if James might already be in hiding. Moments later I know the worst. William goes round the back and emerges dragging James by the hair.

I see then that other figures are appearing in the valley, gathering in the area around James's house. My father is gesturing, giving out instructions. A stake is being hammered into the ground with James's own fence hammer. Brushwood is being fetched from his own outbuilding.

I scramble from the tree and start to run along the summit of the Pike, then realise it will take too long. If Robert went down the screes, then so can I. I push my way through the bushes and confront the precipice of pebbles, then settle my feet in front of me, and go.

It is terrifying, but not as terrifying as the scene below. As the stones start to roar and tumble with me, I lose my footing and go thudding along on my shoulder and hip, skinning my elbow, bombarded about the face and arms by pebbles. Far below, a high-pitched screaming has begun. It is a sound I remember well. I used to lie in my bed at night when I was small and listen to it echoing up the valley from Low Back Farm. Before I reach the bottom of the scree, I can smell the smoke.

Chapter 17

I arrive at the bottom with my stockings torn, my kirtle ridden up round my ears and my shoes lost on the way, but if it weren't for the speed at which I arrived, I think the crowd might not have noticed me, they are so engrossed. How quickly word has travelled. Forty or more surround the stake. James, stripped almost naked, is tied to it, struggling furiously. A low, angry grunting comes from his lips now, as he battles with the ropes. His teeth are bared in an awful grimace, but his mouth looks soft and human, too wet to burn.

"Stop!" I scream. "Are you mad? He isn't a heretic!"

My father comes up and puts his arm round me. I feel repulsed. I can only think of this hand hitting Verity, this hand trying to set fire to James. I realise that in the space of a moment some things have changed for ever. Some things

156

that – what? Make it easier to leave? I push the thought away. There is no time for that, no time for the sort of weakness which Robert causes in my mind and limbs.

My father says, "Now now, Beatrice. What a state you're in. Calm down. It's treason for this lad to have defied his liege lord."

"What?" I am incredulous. "That's rubbish, Father. You're not his liege lord. He's a free man, with his own land. I think you've gone mad. Anyway, even if it were treason, you only burn women for that, not men. You hang men. Anyone knows that. Stop. Please stop."

My father clucks his tongue in exasperation. "Beatrice, the laws are there for us to *interpret*. You're a dutiful daughter, and if you prefer him to hang, then I would normally allow it, but I think swift justice is called for on this occasion. Now let's have no more of this!"

The brushwood around James's feet is not properly caught yet. Sparks like tiny insects run to and fro along the green twigs. I turn away from my father and barge through the crowd and into the pyre, scattering brushwood right and left. The crowd stands in startled silence for a moment, then mutters and moves towards me. I wrench at the knots round James's middle, which attach him to the stake. There is a sort of huffing noise behind me, something strange, not like anything I have ever heard before. I half turn, and realise, in perhaps the most chilling moment of my life, that it is the sound of the crowd, rushing at me.

They grab me. I am too shocked to resist. I find myself pulled to and fro between muscular, hostile hands. "He has bewitched her too!" someone shrieks. "Tie her! Tie her!" I wrench my head round to see the shrieker. It is Tilly Turner, whose house I have been helping rebuild.

"Heee! Heee!" She seems completely mad, and the madness is spreading to others. Mouths are stretched wide with hatred. Eyes are narrowed and vicious. For a moment I almost grasp some truth – something to do with poverty – then Father is elbowing his way to me and it is gone.

"That's enough!" he bellows. He shoves people out of the way and grabs me by the arm. "Get to the tower, girl." He shakes me. The crowd backs off and titters. I cannot tell if he is drunk but his look is suddenly one I can remember from long ago, from sitting on his knee as a small child by another fire, before the ale brought him to his knees and to this one.

I am shaking. My bruises and grazes from coming down the scree are hurting, and I have new scratches and pulled muscles from this rough handling. I shrug free of him, and say, "Father, I'm going to finish untying James." James is rocking to and fro, trying to free himself. I move carefully back among the brushwood and once again try to undo the knots.

"Let's be done with this nonsense," someone calls out.

"Aye, we're wasting time."

"Get that fire lit again."

There are some voices of dissent, though, and I realise that not everyone favours this burning. I call over my shoulder, "Help me. Someone come and help me." Suddenly Leo's wife, Sanctity Wilson, nine months pregnant, is next to me, struggling with the knots that tie James's hands behind him.

"They're a right bugger on your nails, these," she says to me, and grins. Since neither of us has nails to speak of, after all the housebuilding, I take her remark to be a slightly satirical sign of friendship, a way of saying that I may be that stuck-up Beatrice from the tower, but on this occasion, as far as she is concerned, I may consider myself one of them.

James presses back against the stake to make it easier for me to undo the ropes. I tell him, "We'll have you free in a minute." I can feel the warmth round my own ankles from the extinguished sticks, and am suddenly overcome by the terrible human truth of burning, that flesh fries and blood boils. My own nails bend as I fumble faster, trying to disentangle the complicated knots. I am terrified by the thought that the fire might reignite of its own accord, and surge up my skirts and engulf me. One of the knots is undone now. I pull part of the rope loose, but my father suddenly seizes me by the shoulders and drags me backwards, off my feet.

"You are an undutiful daughter, Beatrice," he shouts, and swings his hand at me.

I duck, and struggle to regain my footing. "And you,

sir, are a highway robber," I stammer. His hand stays where it is. We look into each other's eyes. I give a slight nod. I feel changed, freed from something, grown-up perhaps, grown into myself.

"Would you truly betray your father?" he asks in disbelief.

I do not know, and am not called on to reply, because there is a commotion at the edge of the crowd now, and Martinus and George are there, pushing people aside. Their faces are contorted with disgust. At the same moment Parson Becker's horse appears out of the woods beyond the tower, galloping flat out.

John jumps off his horse before it stops, and Universe goes cantering on, propelled by his own speed. I see to my astonishment that our priest has a bullwhip in his hand. Without a word, he sets about the crowd with it. He is more frightening than anything I have ever seen, including the Scots.

The homesteaders back away, screaming. He does not stop until they are scattered over a large area of the valley floor. My father is stepping back and forth as though crazed. He raises his fist, then subsides, looking merely puzzled. At last John lets the whip coil in on itself at his feet. His face is shining with sweat. He looks round and says, "My friends, I have lost patience with you." I think we had rather come to that conclusion ourselves.

After a moment in which we all wait to see what he will do next, he adds, "What is the matter with you all? Truly, what is the matter with you? Do I waste my breath Sunday after Sunday?" then to Tilly Turner, "Untie James."

James is now trying to untie himself, but his hands are shaking so much that he cannot make much headway. He looks on the verge of passing out. Tilly and I untie him, avoiding each other's eyes. John Becker catches him as he falls among the sharp branches. "Come on, James," he says. "I think you and Verity had better stay with me while Cedric patches you both up." He whistles, and Universe comes trotting through the crowd as it disperses along the valley.

Later that day Mother and I drive Verity and James to Wraithwaite Parsonage in the carretta pulled by Saint Hilda. They make a bedraggled pair, jolting together painfully as our little cart lurches along the bumpy tracks. Verity's face is mottled and swollen. Her lips are like cooked beetroot, and both her eyes are blackened. Her shoulder was badly dislocated and has been reset and bound up by Cedric. She keeps weeping in bouts of delayed shock, and can scarcely stand unaided. James has now fallen completely silent. I remember him like this as a child. He will not allow anyone to tend his bruises and grazes. John puts him to bed in the small room behind the hearth, because it has a lock on the door, and he believes that James needs this extra feeling of security just now. Mother stays with Verity in the austere, wood-panelled guestroom upstairs. As I am leaving, John takes my hands and says, "We need to speak together." I feel a leap of fright in my throat, then realise that he can't possibly know about Robert. I nod, abruptly light-hearted. Yes, when all this is over, we can sit down and talk. It will be wonderful, like the old days in the classroom, when anything could be discussed and no problems were insoluble.

Through the hot days of late July, and into August, Verity does not return. I miss her. I feel I have lost her, and that it is my own fault. I did not appreciate her when I had her. I neglected her by concentrating on Robert.

I try to reverse that. I stay away from Robert and spend more time at Wraithwaite Parsonage. It is clear that John is talking to Verity and James about their futures, and trying to assess whether love as well as convenience is involved in Verity's plan. He will not allow my father over the threshold. He has taken Mother Bain on as his housekeeper. Cedric is often there too. He seems to be surrounding himself with magic.

My father is angry all the time now. He is sometimes away for nights on end, roaming, we assume, to more distant highways, and though we dread to think what he is doing, his absence is a relief. When he is home, he accuses us of all manner of disloyalties. He accused George and Martinus of treason against him, and dismissed them without pay. He accused me of making a fool of him in front of the homesteaders. He accused my mother of undermining his authority by riding over to fetch the priest on the day of the burning, as indeed she did. She, in her turn, treats him with contempt.

As the heat and humidity build up, Robert is frequently angry too. This English summer is too hot for him. He is bored, and I can see he is miserable that I stay away so much. When I do go, he is so beautiful and well-looking, yet so foreign, that it feels more frightening and wrong than ever. His strength returns, and as I see what he has become, I realise how close to death he must have been before. We lie by the beck and talk, and I feel closer to him than I do to what remains of my own family. We edge closer and closer to meaning too much to each other, so that I am afraid of the moment when a parting will become unbearable. We touch more and more, kiss cheeks and hair and foreheads at any excuse, become shy of each other's bodies in a way that I was not shy of his when I nursed him.

In mid August, harvest time, the summons comes to prepare to join the border lords' retributive raid on Scotland. I think we had all hoped that it would be quietly forgotten. Certainly no one has mentioned it for weeks, through the long, sultry hours of mowing, raking, rick-building and planting for winter, when these practical matters of life have taken our minds right away from practical prospects of death.

We take on Tilly Turner to work in the dairy. Mother has vowed to knock some sense into her if it kills them both. We are all too hot, and short of patience, much of the time. Kate and Germaine gossip for hours sprawled on the kitchen settle in the evenings, drinking ale and sweating with the dying heat of the cooking fire on top of the heat of the day. When the call comes for all able-bodied men to prepare to march against the Scots, their talk takes on a new, gloomier tone. Although Germaine puts a good face on it and says what is expected of her, conventional declarations about hoping our men beat the living daylights out of the Scots, I sense real dread in her, an uncontrollable fear that Gerald might not come back.

One hot, deep day with thunder threatening, I take the familiar path through the forest. The tracks are very overgrown now, after all the sun and rain. Pushing through them is increasingly difficult. The blackberries and hazelnuts are ripening profusely in this lost part of the woods. Soon people will come here, hacking through the brambles and undergrowth, to stock up for winter. It is time for Robert to go.

He is not at the cottage when I arrive. He is often out trapping in the woods, so I settle down to wait. As always, I wonder if this time he has gone for good, and I face the fact that one day he *will* have gone for good. The thought fills me with despair.

It is so hot that my clothes are sticking to my back. I loosen my bodice and walk to the beck, just out of sight of the cottage. I lie down on the cool moss and damp stones, and close my eyes.

"Beatrice!"

I must have been dozing. The warm, fuddled moment of relief turns to icy dismay.

"John..."

John Becker emerges from the trees. He is wearing loose, light, peasant's clothing, his linen shirt open at the neck. I am speechless.

"How nice to see you, Beatrice. I hadn't expected to meet anyone in such a remote part of the woods."

"I..."

"Have you just been walking here?"

"Yes..."

"I find that walking in the woods helps me think clearly. Do you find that?"

"Yes, I..."

There is a rustling of twigs. I have time enough to feel sick with dread, seconds in which my mind races to find a way to warn Robert to stay back, be silent, before an elegant figure emerges from the greenery like some sort of nymph. "We are here to see how the cobnuts are ripening," says Germaine, her dainty face scarlet with heat. "Are we not, mistress?"

I nod. I feel faint. I sit down on a fallen tree trunk.

"It does look like a good harvest." John glances round at the laden hazel trees with their delicately fringed nuts in great, tight clusters. He reaches up and touches some which hang near his face. "Not quite ready yet, I think."

Germaine looks at them critically. "Nay sir, you're right. We shall have to return another day, I daresay."

He smiles at us. "Well, it's good to see you."

Germaine drops him a curtsey, by way of dismissal, and with a last look at me, John leaves. For a while we can hear his progress through the woods. It seems infinitely appealing that he is so noisy, that here is someone who doesn't need to be silent and creep about.

"He means you. He means it's good to see you." Germaine leans against a tree trunk and gazes at me. "You could have that one if you wanted."

I don't know whether to laugh or cry. "Germaine, for heaven's sake..."

"Quite." She is laughing.

I stand up, but find that my legs are still too weak with fright to hold me, and sit back down with a bump.

"Beatrice, my dear." Germaine crosses to me and kisses my cheek. "I'll be off now, and leave you to it. I never thought you had it in you. Snibbed by a Scot, lady. I can forgive you a lot for such unsurpassed indiscretion." She swings round, her skirts missing the briars in a way that mine would not have, and tramps away through the forest, laughing.

Chapter 18

The wind is rising, taking the edge off the heat, and long shadows surround the cottage by the time Robert returns. I am sitting on a rock with my feet in the beck, eating part of a dry loaf from the day before. I watch his approach down the slope at the far side of the stream. Two rabbits hang from his hand. He is barefoot. He steps down the steep bank and wades through the water, curling his toes on the slippery stones. He reaches me and stops. "I'll just put these in the meat safe," he says, and touches my hair with his free hand.

I think of all the little snares out in the woods, set to catch the unwary, the rabbits and birds who do not see the invisible noose, the hidden hinge, until the trap is sprung, and it is too late. How easy it is to be caught.

Robert has constructed a tightly woven willow cage and hung it in the shade at the back of the cottage, for storing surplus food. He could live here, I think. He could live here for ever, if it were not for the increasing risk of discovery by others besides Germaine. I wonder how I am going to face her, plead with her to keep my secret. I dread to think what she has seen and heard while she has been spying on us.

I get up and follow Robert round the back of the cottage. He is batting away flies from the outside of the meat safe, before putting the rabbits in. He looks over his shoulder at me. I feel as if he knows what I am going to say.

"Robert, it's time to go. There were people here earlier, the priest and a servant from the tower. It isn't safe any more. The tides will be right for crossing by the end of the month."

He is silent, putting the rabbits away, then he says, "Aye, I daresay you're right."

"I'll smuggle you down to the shore under cover of darkness, but it's too dangerous to cross the sands at night. You can hide in one of the caves until first light, then Cedric can take you over."

"Beatrice..."

I put my hand over his lips. "Don't."

He holds my hand there, in his, then removes it and keeps hold of it. "I could live here, you know. We manage, don't we."

I look at him. Increasingly we echo one another's

thoughts. I press his hand to my own mouth, then let go of it. "They'd catch you. You can't pretend to be dumb for ever."

We walk back to the beck, and take turns drinking from a flagon of elderflower cordial which I have brought. He says, "I suppose I've merely become dependent on you, Beatrice. That's all it is. Ridiculous to think I cannae cope without you. Of course I bluidy can." He kneels at the beck and lifts handfuls of water to wet his face and hair. I wish I could warn him about the march on Scotland, explain that this is why he must be well on his way as soon as possible. Talk is of little else at the tower. Aunt Juniper is prostrate with panic at the thought of Hugh and Gerald going to fight. She attempted briefly to organise a campaign against the edict of the border lords, until she was warned by Magistrate Chantry that defiance of this sort would be regarded as a breach of the peace, particularly since the queen herself is said to have given unspoken blessing to the raid.

Father is to lead the march northwards, despite the general feeling that he might not remain vertical beyond the end of the valley. Perhaps his breath will be enough to fell Scottish castle walls. My mind is churning as Robert and I watch the sun go down between the trees in slivers of blood-red. The low light shines through the moss on the north sides of the tree trunks, and through the small hairs on his arms. There is a feeling of finality between us, and of the recklessness which finality brings. I ask,

"Robert, are you angry with me?"

"Aye." He turns to look at me, then leans over and kisses me slowly on the mouth. My bones melt at the prospect of just going with it, letting it happen. He seems to sense my wavering, moves his lips to my throat and presses them to the place where my bodice is still unlaced. We have never done this before, never got this far. I know the countryside is full of people with their skirts up and their breeches down, but for Robert and me, until now, the mere existence of our relationship has been transgression enough. He raises his head and looks at me. I hold his face away. It's no good. He has to go, and this would make it worse. I say, "We have to stop."

"No we don't." He kisses me again so that I fall back in the bracken and knock my head on a rock. He says, "Sorry, sorry, Beatrice. Bea. Look, please come with me. Truly. You must come with me. We're not savages. Scotland is so lovely. You don't want to marry Hugh, do you. You said so. Your family is a disaster. What's to keep you here?"

I roll away from him. The crushed bracken releases a wave of raw, green perfume like an exhalation of sadness. I tell him, "You're the enemy, Robert. What if your people or mine ever invaded each other again?"

He pulls me back, and leans over me, propped on his hands. Water from his hair drips on to my face. He says, "I think I fell in love with you that first day, when I saw you standing guard on the Pike. You heard us, didn't you, even though we were a fair way off down the slope, hiding amongst the trees and barely making a sound. You made us move sharpish that day, Beatrice, I can tell you, coming striding round the edge of the woods like that, with your knife and your fierce look."

"So you *were* there. Oh dear God, Robert. What would you have done if I'd found you? Killed me?"

There is a moment of horror between us, a silence which cannot be filled. Then I wrap my arms round his head and pull him close.

I stay until the sun has gone, lying in Robert's arms, stroking his hair, touching the jagged red scar that disfigures his healed arm. We kiss and hold each other, not speaking much, until the bats come from their high crevices and scoop the air round our heads with their wings. Then I walk home in darkness, just another shadow amongst the foxes and badgers.

Early in the morning I walk down to the shore to look for the Cockleshell Man. Rabbits and sheep are feeding below the cliffs. They scatter as I walk down the stony path and head out into the bay, jumping some of the low-tide pools. I can see Cedric far out beyond the grassline, planting clumps of eelgrass in the sand's wrinkled surface, to mark the safe way across the bay. Breaks in the line mean that the quicksand has shifted, and that the eelgrass has gone where you will go if you step there.

The calling of the sheep becomes fainter as I walk

further out, following Cedric's earlier footsteps in the sand. I look back and see the rabbits I disturbed foraging again under the cliffs. Could I leave all this? I look at the possibility seriously for the first time.

Cedric has been scraping cockles out of the sand. Watery sunlight reflects off the piles of shellfish, and off his shiny leather back. He straightens up from his planting, stretching with his hands in the small of his back. "Beatrice, have you come to be my pupil?"

I grimace. "Sorry, Cedric. I don't think I'm ready for maggots yet."

He laughs. "You will be. I have high hopes of you. How is your Scot?"

"Much better, thank you. Ready to go."

"Aye well, the tides will be right in three days." He gazes across the bay. "Pity he can't go today, being Sunday, when the holy are likely to have their minds on higher things."

"I thought I'd bring him down to the shore during the night and hide him in one of the caves until there's enough light to cross by. Can we find him a horse?"

"I'll get him one at Cartmel. He'll be better crossing the sands on foot. A missing horse would raise the alarm." He is threading and knotting his nets now. Each hempen net has loose ropes at all four corners, which he will tie in twos to black wooden stakes driven deep into the sand. When the tide comes in, fish are washed into the nets. When it flows out again, they are trapped. They make the same mistake that I have made.

Cedric stops knotting and looks at me. "It's hard for you, isn't it."

"Yes."

"Best get back. Tide's coming."

"Yes."

A whisper of wind dulls the sand and there is the taste of salt on my tongue. We talk some more, planning the fine details of Robert's escape, then I walk back, leaving the Cockleshell Man to tie the last of his nets and beat the tide. He will not be caught. He knows the bay and its timing too well. At the top of the cliff path I look back, and see a distant glint of water at the mouth of the bay, and a small figure making his way inland with sacks of cockles over his back. Ahead of me in the woods the rowan and blackthorn are changing colour early this year, and the bracken is edged blood-brown.

Now I have to deal with Germaine. She could ruin everything. She and Kate are spending much of their time making preparations for a feast we are to hold for the men marching on Scotland, and just a casual word of gossip between them could be Robert's death sentence. Later that Sunday morning she and I emerge from church together. We walk along the sun-cracked path to the trough on Wraithwaite Green where our horses are tethered. I glance at her and say, "He's going. Please don't say anything. He's going very soon."

"Is he indeed."

"Please tell me... do you intend giving us away, Germaine?"

She slots her tiny foot into the stirrup and mounts her pony, hooking her right knee over the leather support and arranging her skirts in a leisurely way. "Beatrice, I don't know what you propose to do. I don't want to know. I shall not be sorry to see you go north, if you do go. Others have gone, they say. You are too arrogant for my taste. But no, I shall not speak to anyone. I'll say this to you though, if you've done dallying with the Scotsman, you'd be better off taking the priest." She jerks her chin in the direction of the church's sunlit porch where John is having what looks like a hostile discussion with my father. "He's arrogant and self-righteous too. You'd suit each other. What is there – ten years between you? It's nothing." She clicks her tongue and taps her pony across the neck with a loop of rein, and adds, "I wish you well, Beatrice. Don't ask me to help you, but I'll not harm you."

I watch her go, then sit down abruptly on the edge of the stone trough. Verity and James, who left church early to avoid my father, have now re-emerged from the parsonage and are coming over to join me. I watch them walking and laughing, easy with each other.

I wave and they wave back. At the church John is now talking to Master Spearing. He looks in my direction and smiles. I remember the faces of the crowd at the burning. I wonder, am I arrogant? Am I perhaps so dislikeable, so

174

disliked here, that I might be better off elsewhere, having a fresh start? I nod and smile at some of my neighbours from the valley who are beginning the long walk home, and I try not to appear gracious or patronising, but have no means of knowing whether I succeed. Perhaps I do need to talk to Germaine more, though her remarks about John are clearly ridiculous. Somehow she must have realised that I used to daydream about him when I was younger, before I knew that someone like Robert could undermine all commonsense and reason.

The sun goes behind a cloud and a cold wind blows, a first hint of autumn. I feel raw and unpredictable, like the weather. I want to be honest in my telling of events, to portray us all with truth and fairness, yet today I'm not sure that I see even myself clearly enough to be able to comment on anyone else. I pull Saint Hilda towards me and hook my arm under her big warm face, and rest my cheek against it.

Chapter 19

The valley is full of strangers these days. Men are gathering from surrounding areas for the march on Scotland. A long table and benches stand outside the gatehouse, and Kate hands out bread, cheese and ale there, as new people arrive. In less than a week they will leave for Newcastle, and a fortnight from now men from all over the northern counties will march out of Newcastle to repay old debts.

My father is trying to stay off the drink. He looks grey and sick. Everywhere people are unusually irritable, with a tendency to weep unexpectedly. Anti-Scottish feeling is running high. Robert must go quickly now.

On the day of the leaving feast I go to the cottage just before dawn, to remind Robert that I will take him down to the shore some time around midnight, when everyone is too drunk to notice, though I doubt he needs reminding, since nothing else is on our minds at the moment. He is not there. I feel angry with him, and sad. How much time does he think we still have, that he can go jaunting off into the forest without me? I wait a while, then leave the food I brought and return to the tower. Today, with hectic preparations for the feast, my absence would certainly be noticed.

Kate and a group of valley women have been working for two days preparing food. The long table in the living hall has been moved over and the one from outside brought up the east stairs to join it. Another, smaller table has been borrowed from the women's common room to place across the top, as high table for the family. People start arriving outside from midday onwards, and in the late afternoon we open the door and let them in.

Despite the heat, fires have been lit at both ends of the living hall. Homesteaders, farmers and villagers settle themselves elbow to elbow, back to back, knee to knee, along the benches at the two long tables, those nearest the fires sweating into their ale as soon as they sit down. Verity and James arrive with John Becker. Aunt and Uncle Juniper arrive with Hugh and Gerald. At six o'clock I accompany the rest of the family up the east stairs and into the living hall. We have dressed in our best, to honour the fighters. I am wearing a padded russet kirtle over my red silk gown, now miraculously restored by Germaine, who gave it an impressed stare and muttered something about some people really knowing how to enjoy themselves.

We make our way to the carved oak chairs at the high table, and encounter the full blast of heat thrown out by the fires and the crowd. My father is on my right and John Becker on my left. Hugh is at the far side of my parents, and appears not to be speaking to me. The atmosphere between John and my father is also strained. It's going to be a long evening. I find I don't care. I don't care about any of this, the festivities or the undercurrents. I shall see Robert at midnight, and it will be for the last time.

After prayers have been said for everyone's safe return, my father shouts, "Eat, eat!" Kate and Tilly Turner serve at the top table, but everyone else helps themselves from the wooden platters piled high with mutton, beef, fish, shellfish, buttered turnips, beans in cinnamon honey and great manchets of bread. The heat is almost intolerable. I loosen my collar. Father keeps mopping his brow with his napkin. A few people have already fainted. It seems an oddly fitting part of this farewell feast that bodies should be carried out, tested beyond endurance by the fires and by their fears for those who will, with this same clumsy, stumbling awkwardness, be carried home.

"Best enjoy the heat whilst ye can," says Kate darkly as she bends over Father's shoulder to serve him peach sauce. "It may be colder where you're going."

Next to me, John keeps passing me appetising items of food, and I do the same for him. We seem to be ending up feeding each other, our fingers dripping with grease. I start to relax, and laugh a little. In view of Germaine's daft ideas about him, I feel strange sitting so close, but he clearly thinks nothing of it. I lean back and look round the hall. All along the benches strong young men with bright, healthy faces are exchanging views on their weaponry, in some cases admiring one another's swords and axes which regrettably have been brought to table. Couples are gazing into each other's eyes, facing the prospect of months apart.

I watch Germaine going round lighting the torches in the wall sconces, as the light outside fades. Her face is puffy. She has been crying. Kate lights candles along the tables, and the heat increases even further. A lot of ale, mead and wine is being drunk. The noise of talk and laughter is very loud, and people are losing their inhibitions. Germaine finishes lighting the torches, then comes and sits next to Gerald at the high table. My father rises unsteadily to his feet, stares at her for a moment, then pulls her up to join him in his own chair. Mother, who has been sitting on Father's right, rises to her feet, walks down the hall smiling graciously at those she passes, and squeezes on to the bench next to the Cockleshell Man.

I lean forward and look past Mother's empty place to the end of the table, where Verity, seated between Hugh and James, is working her way systematically through a pile of shellfish. She spits a fragment of shell from her round pink lips and makes a throat-cutting gesture in

179

Cedric's direction. I grin. Suddenly, the past weeks of separation vanish. I feel close to her again, normal. Next to her James murmurs something in her ear, and she laughs. There is a new air of confidence about him these days. I wonder if she will have such a pliant husband as she thinks, if she does eventually marry him. I turn to John. Half way down one of the tables people have started singing. I have to shout in his ear to make him hear. "Verity seems good for James. Is he good for her, do you think?"

John hesitates a moment, holding a piece of bread dipped in peach sauce half way to his lips. He puts it down, and in a lull in the din, says, "To tell you the truth, I'm not sure. Times are changing. Verity's attitude is... I don't know... part of something exciting that's going on in the country. We don't see it so much here, but in the cities there's new music, new writing, new attitudes. Headstrong people like Verity are leading it. I think she'll have her way whether or not it's good for her, and she'll handle the consequences and make it work. She has an overriding desire to own land, and farm it unencumbered by other people's expectations. James won't get in her way, so in that sense he's good for her." He has to raise his voice again as singing breaks out once more. "If it causes a permanent rift with your father, well, that could be bad. They're fond of each other, despite everything."

"If Verity were to marry James, it would change everything that's been planned for the future of Mere Point and here."

"Well, not everything, would it? If you marry Hugh, he could come here, and Gerald could stay at Mere Point and marry whomever he pleased."

"*If* I marry Hugh."

John looks at me quickly. "Is there some doubt?"

Doubt – if only he knew how much doubt. It is nine o'clock. In another two hours I must leave for the cottage. I raise my goblet to him, down some elderberry wine, and say, "Yes, there's doubt."

In the shifting light John's face looks vulnerable and young. He says, after a pause, "There seems to be truth in the air this evening. Beatrice... if there is some doubt that you are to marry Hugh, then..."

Someone leans between us. It is William, one of Father's henchmen. He has to shout above the uproar. "Parson, you're needed, sir. Mistress Mattock's son says to come at once. His mother's been tekken bad wi' t'visions again."

John nods at William. "Thanks. I'll come at once. Does she want the Cockleshell Man too?"

"Nay sir. She reckons as he's in league wi' t'devil."

John stands up and looks down at me. "I'll try to get back later. Beatrice, are we to continue with this conversation, or..." He half smiles. "... am I making a truly humiliating mistake?"

I stand up beside him. Any other night, and yes, I would have had this and any other conversation on earth with him, but tonight I do not know the answer. William looks curiously from one to the other of us. I struggle for words, but John is already turning away, taking my silence as reply. By the time I call after him, "John..." he is making his way down the hall, struggling past slumped bodies and heaps of discarded clothing and weaponry. He has vanished through the door to the spiral staircase long before I can reach him.

Chapter 20

I have lost my appetite. As the evening wears on I sip wine, and speak to people as little as possible, waiting for midnight to draw closer. Time seems to have slowed. Some of the torches go out but the fires flare high and brassy at each end of the hall, and the shadows in between leap tall and wild. I have been up since before dawn. I am very tired. People blend in and out of my vision. All along the tables guests shout, laugh, sob, drop their tankards and fall off benches.

"Sing, Kate!" someone shouts. "Sing us a battle song!"

The uproar subsides a little. Kate's voice is renowned throughout the valley and beyond. She climbs up on to the table next to me, clumsy with her bad leg. She half tips over the great silver salt, and I steady it, my eyes following the inscription dizzyingly round its rim, *The*

183

rose is redde, the leafe is greene, God save Elizabeth our queene. I rub my eyes to get rid of the dazzle, and sit back, glad that Kate is going to sing, glad that I don't have to talk to anyone for a while.

They asked for a battle song, but Kate sings a lament. Her voice rises pure and ghostly along the length of the hall, and silences everyone. When the last verse dies away, full of words about not returning, someone starts weeping loudly in a corner, and others cough and shuffle their feet. I half rise to ask Kate to sing something more cheerful, but as I do, from the far end of the second table, another voice starts up. It is a resonant male voice, controlled and powerful. It sings *Mistress mine well may you fare* with a sure and light-footed perfection of pitch. It transfixes me to my chair. The singer is in shadow. His voice fills the hall. Everyone listens in silence.

"In these woods are none that hurt,
Men can speak but silent words..."

He has chosen well.

"Who's yon?" mutters someone near me.

"One of t'new henchmen I reckon. Them as replaced George and Martinus."

"That's right," I agree hurriedly, edging out of my chair. I am no longer hot. I am so cold that I am shivering. I squeeze behind my father and Verity, and make my way down the hall, pushing between the wall and the backs of people. No one takes any notice of me. They are too intent on this new singer with his beautiful voice. I trip over guests who are lying on the floor, and push past those huddled in the corners created by the square stone pillars. Oh Robert, I thought I knew you so well, but I didn't know you could sing.

It is quite dark at the centre of the hall. At the door which leads to the spiral staircase I come up against my mother.

"Whatever can have got into Cedric?" she asks plaintively, waving a goblet of French wine at me. "He just jumped up and went off." She prods a prone henchman with her foot.

"He'll be back, Mother," I assure her, whilst wondering which of us will indeed be back this night.

The singer is on his last verse now. He is standing where light from the far fire only reaches intermittently. I make my way round the end of the first table and past the fire. I can see him now. He has one foot on the bench and one on the table. As I reach the second table the song ends, and a cheer goes up. People around him reach over and slap his legs in approval.

"More!"

"That's more like it!"

"Mistresses we want, not graveyards, ye old baggage," someone yells at Kate. With no further encouragement the stranger begins the *Robin Hood Round*. As with any round, it is an invitation to others to join in, and Kate's voice comes in powerfully above the stranger's. I put my hands on my hips and look up at him. Robert looks down at me and smiles. A few people notice me and raise their tankards.

Other voices are coming in now, adding more parts to the round, and some confusion too, but Kate's and Robert's voices keep the tune going until they finally arrive at the same note at the same time, and both burst out laughing in triumph, while all the rest trail off in disarray.

"There's a man after my own heart," shouts Kate.

"You'd better get out now, while you can," I whisper to him.

"Not without you." Robert's voice is also quiet, then he goes straight into the first verse of *The Willow Tree*. I jump, as a plucking music begins at the other end of the hall, and realise that in honour of this strange singer, Germaine has extricated herself from my father's grip and is playing her lute. She plays this considerably better than she plays the fiddle, and the resulting music is powerful and affecting, all the more so when Kate joins in again. A few others join in too, humming the verses or singing the choruses. I stand there helplessly, wondering how long before people, drunk as they are, notice the other thing in this singer's voice, a Scottish accent.

It happens the next moment. The song ends. Another cheer goes up. People stamp their feet and clank their tankards and drum their hands on the tables.

"More!"

"Sing a mucky song! Go on! Sing t'nightingale song!"

But my father, perhaps angry at the loss of Germaine's comforting weight, shouts from the far end of the hall, "Who's that? Who are you? Show yourself, singer. I'll have no travelling balladeers in here. Spies, every one of 'em!"

A quietness falls on the gathering. In the silence, a log in the far hearth caves in with a sigh, and a puff of smoke and sparks billows out into the room. I move quickly towards the door to the spiral staircase. It opens slightly as I reach it, and I see Cedric outside, beckoning. "I've saddled a horse," he whispers. I nod, and turn back to where Robert has stepped down into the firelight between the tables.

"Greetings." His voice is not raised, but the stillness is now such that it echoes all round the hall. "I thought I'd come and see you at your Anglo-Saxon revelry."

An incredulous ripple runs the length of the tables.

"By God! A Scot!"

In the paralysis which follows, Robert calls, "Aye, and what a pathetic sight you all make. You poor drunken sots think you'll be invading Queen Mary's royal Scotland? It's laughable. I don't know whether to laugh or cry. I suggest ye dinnae bother. For one thing you'll no be capable, and for another, I'm away to warn them."

He jumps with both bare feet on to the table, and runs along it, knocking down plates, trenchers, food and tankards. People draw back with shrieks, as legs of mutton land in their laps, and cascades of ale spray their bosoms. When he is level with the door where I stand, he leaps again, over heads, to reach it. Yes Robert, I certainly appear to have mended you all right.

He is through the door and running downstairs, taking the steps three at a time, even as the assembly rises with a roar and charges after him.

"After him! He can't get far!"

"Catch the bugger! He's here to spy for Scotland!"

"I warned you... travelling balladeers..."

"Get him! Fetch your bratch-hounds, Master Spearing."

They all run the way Robert has gone, down the spiral staircase, tumbling and falling and holding on to the walls. I run the other way, down the straight stairs behind the eastern fireplace, to my room, then on down the silent, empty stone steps which lead past the kitchen to the underground passage and the barmkin. Pray God no one has opened the wolf-pit. I have no time to bother with candles or lanterns. In less than a minute I am up through the floor of the dairy and out into the barmkin. At the front of the tower, shouting and bellowing, the assembled neighbourhood comes crashing out into the night.

It is dark. There are clouds obscuring the moon and stars — good for Robert, bad for me just now. I can sense the horses shifting about, unnerved by the commotion. I make my way to the corner where Saint Hilda usually stands. Something touches my ankle, Caesar my cat, also out hunting. Saint Hilda is there, but someone is on her

188

back, and someone else is holding her head, two silent black shapes, very still, waiting to see who is approaching them. I am filled with fury.

"How *dare* you come here? Get *away* from my horse, Scotsman!"

"How dare *I*?" It is Robert on the horse, his voice filled with bitterness. "Why didn't you *tell* me? I had tae hear about this bluidy raid from a couple of riders out in the forest."

Saint Hilda shies, reacting to his tone. The Cockleshell Man steadies his grip on her head as the rein whips through his fingers. He soothes her, whispering in her ear, then he says to Robert, "Tell you? How could she tell you? Do you think she's a traitor to her own people just because she helped you the way she'd help a wounded dog?" He turns to me. "Beatrice, let him take your horse. I'll ride with him. I've saddled your father's horse too. Just open the barmkin gate when I say, then get back to your room."

I hesitate. The sound of the crowd is growing nearer as they come round the tower wall, searching for a trail, spreading out as they come. "No." I hitch my skirts above my knees. "You open the gate, Cedric. I'll ride with Robert on Saint Hilda. You follow on Caligula. We'll need you to see us across the bay." With one foot on the mounting block I vault on to Saint Hilda's broad back, behind Robert, and click my tongue. "Come on girl, down to the shore." I look at Cedric, who is holding my father's horse, Caligula. "Can we beat the tide, Cedric?"

He sniffs the air. "Maybe. One way. Is that what you want?"

The crowd is coming. There is no time. Cedric flings open the barmkin gate. Robert lurches and grasps the reins. I hold him round the waist and kick at Saint Hilda's sides. She sets off at a fast running trot, under the stone arch, then breaks into a gallop as she feels open country ahead, and the familiar road down to the sea. Behind us, a cry goes up. Closer, I can hear the slap of Caligula's hooves on turf.

When I am sure that Robert has good control of the horse, I look behind me. The moon comes out, and I can see Cedric outlined against the white tower, on Father's black horse. Close behind him, terrifyingly close, comes the crowd, running.

"There he goes!"

"Catch him!"

"Whip t'bugger off his horse!"

The disjointed phrases come to me on the wind. Then there is a different sound, a pulsating whistle, a throbbing in the air, a loud crack, and a faint, fading cry. When I look back, Cedric is no longer on his horse. What I heard was a bullwhip. They have whipped him off his horse. Caligula still follows behind us, running wild, his eyes pale and bulging, his gallop slowing. Then they are all out of sight, and the steep side of the Pike is rushing by in a blur.

Carried on the wind – or is it only in my head? – I hear a voice. "Mind the tide, Beatrice. Mind the tide."

Chapter 21

"They thought Cedric was you, Robert. They whipped him off his horse," I shout against his back as we reach the trees and the cliff path.

Robert reins in. "Dear God! We'd better get back. They'll kill him if they know he helped me."

"They won't know. He'll say he was chasing you. No, we've got to go on now. We'll barely make it as it is."

He hesitates, and Saint Hilda edges towards the cliff path, which is where she had thought she was going. Robert tightens the reins and turns to look at me. "Well you'd better get back anyhow, Beatrice. Join the merry throng. Pretend you were never away. They have no reason to connect you with me." He holds on to the reins with his bad arm and puts his good one round me. "Thank you, dearest girl. I shall never forget you. I trust I was a little more than the wounded dog Cedric seems to think me."

"You know you were. Come on. We'd better get on down the path. You'll never cross the sands on your own."

There is a longer silence than we can afford.

"You're coming with me?"

"Yes."

"Just across the sands?"

"Yes."

"I'll not have that. You don't know the way either, and in darkness too..."

I unwind his arm from round me and kiss the back of his neck. "I've crossed before. I'll do my best. It's your only hope of getting away. They'll be after you on horseback and with hounds in the time it takes to saddle up and wake the dogs. You can't go round the bay. It would take too long and they'd cut you off. Your only hope is to cross before the next tide. By the time the tide is out again, your tracks will have gone, and you'll have had time to get on northwards." I look at the moon and try to reckon what time of night it is. If it is close enough to the incoming tide, our pursuers will not risk following us out on to the sands. I dismount. "Here, let me ride in front. There's somewhere we must go first."

"First? What do you mean? There's no time."

I jump up in front of him, whirling my foot over Saint Hilda's head and taking the reins from him. I grip with my knees and guide her down the dark, rocky path which leads to the sea. Half way down I turn off to the left. At that moment, in the distance, comes the starved baying of loosed hounds, Master Spearing's bratch-hounds. I remember Mad Joly's teeth in my face, and the hairs rise on the back of my neck.

"Mary and all the saints," mutters Robert. "Where are we going, Beatrice? This doesn't seem the way to the sea."

"We must go to the chapel first, Robert. We have to ask for a safe crossing. The last travellers who didn't went down in the quicksand."

I kick Saint Hilda into a precipitous canter along the twisting, sloping track. Robert holds firmly on to me. I can feel his breath on my neck. Tree branches lash our heads and stones shoot away from under Saint Hilda's hooves. We emerge into a clearing where the chapel stands on the cliff edge, brilliant white in the moonlight. Through the trees the damp sand stretches away to Gewhorn Head, and a broad, broken strip of light shines from one side to the other, like a pathway to safety.

"At least the moon's out, thank God," I whisper. We dismount, and I lead the way into the tiny, rudimentary stone building, reconsecrated by Parson Becker after the last carter was hanged for robbing people. The low, salt-rimed doorway is hung with spiders' webs. Clearly no one has crossed the sands for weeks. The door creaks on its hinges and the webs wrap themselves round our heads as we enter. Far off, the dogs howl.

"Dear God, Beatrice, is this really necessary?" Robert whispers.

"And you call *me* a heathen. Come on."

Inside, instead of an altar facing east, a water-bleached wooden table faces west, with a view across the bay through three unglazed arched windows. I kneel hastily in front of it, clasp my hands on the warped grey wood and stare out of the window. "Please save us from the dogs, the people and the tide." Robert utters a fervent amen, then we are through the door and away.

"They'll think you've gone by the other path," I shout back at him. "They won't expect you to know about the chapel and this way down." We reach the bottom of the cliff. I have been frantically trying to work out the tides, in my head. It must still be well before midnight. The tide is quite obviously out, but how long has it been gone? How long will it be before it turns, and comes rushing back, faster than a galloping horse? Last high tide was around midday, so next high tide will be around midnight, or just after. There should be time to cross, just, but hardly time for me to get back. By that time my absence will probably have been discovered anyway.

As we pick our way between the low tide pools on the grassy foreshore, there is a sudden crescendo of barking and yelping at the top of the cliff, curdling away into a series of howls. Seconds later the sounds of human voices and horses' hooves can be heard. I had been going to suggest to Robert that we send Saint Hilda back, and cross on foot, rather than risk my horse out on the quicksands. Slowness and caution are necessary anyway, and a horse would be no advantage without a knowledgeable guide making speed possible. Now we have no choice. I kick at Saint Hilda's flanks and she leaps forward over the salt pools with her loping stride, until we come to the wide, wet sands.

Robert is silent behind me. I lean back into his comforting warmth, and we settle to a steady trot, keeping to the clumps of eelgrass which trail off into the moonlit distance. I know, anyway, how to recognise the danger spots, though they are harder to see at night. The sand shimmers smooth and silky where water is trapped in it. The places we need to tread are dull and ridged. I guide my patient horse's head to and fro on the dull, ridged, safe patches of sand, and think what under-appreciated qualities dullness and safety are. Behind us a shout echoes and rebounds round the cliffs. "There he goes!" In the night air, the voices carry clearly.

"God help him. He's crossing the sands. No call to chase after him now, then. Fasten the dogs."

"Hold on! There's two on t'horse. He's tekking someone. We'd best get after him."

"Nay, Master Spearing." Whose voice? Germaine's, I think. "You're drunk. You're seeing double. There's just the Scot."

The voices fade into a garbled echo and soon we can no longer hear them. I slow Saint Hilda's pace, and Robert tightens his hold on me. We ride in silence for a while. Suddenly, the eelgrass ends, and bare sand stretches

195

ahead. At the same moment the first breath of sea breeze blows gently against our faces. I tense, and I can feel Robert also tensing behind me, but I dare not go faster for fear of missing our footing, now that the safe way is no longer marked.

"Why did you do it, Robert?" I ask him, over my shoulder, slowing Saint Hilda, picking my way. "Why did you come to the tower? It was mad."

He rubs his face in my hair. "I think I was mad. I had to see you. I was so angry. You deceived me, and I wanted to see you in your tower again, I suppose because that was the place where you'd been my enemy before. I felt you must be a different person from what I'd thought. You hadnae told me about the raid. I had to overhear it from two hunters in the forest, and one of them your Cousin Hughie. I was just so angry with you, Beatrice. I wanted to shock and frighten you..."

"Well you did that all right." I turn on him, angry myself. "Don't forget what you did, Robert. Don't forget that *you* raided *us*, unprovoked. One of our men died because of you."

"It's what we do though, isn't it Bea. It's just what we all do. Your people, my people. Don't let's part angry. I'm very sorry that I've put you in such danger. I can see now that there was nothing else you could do..." He does not finish, because suddenly Saint Hilda's front hooves give way. I had lost concentration. She pitches forward with a terrified whinny, and I realise that we are into quicksand.

"Get off!" I yell at Robert. I tumble off, and Robert jumps down behind me. Saint Hilda steadies a little, now that our weight is off, but continues struggling to free herself, working herself further into the morass as she does so.

The breath is shocked out of me, but I try to speak soothingly to her, as between us we seize whatever parts of her we can. Robert has her tail and I have her mane. I wind my fist into it and pull, and tufts of warm, coarse hair come loose in my hands. I clasp my arms round her neck, and she wheezes in terror, baring her teeth, half choking. It is difficult finding a footing ourselves, but slowly we begin to reclaim her. In dismay, I see in the moonlight the sloppy, shifting surface edging closer to where Robert and I have a temporary footing. My own feet are starting to become embedded. With a grunt, Robert stoops and puts his shoulder under Saint Hilda's belly. Slowly he pushes with his back, and slowly the horse's legs suck free. Now Robert is sinking. I hook his arm into the stirrup – his bad arm is the only one which will reach – and back Saint Hilda on to firmer ground. Her eyes roll and her lips curl back in a grimace, as Robert's weight threatens to pull her down, but when she realises she can lift her feet freely again, she slowly calms and stops blowing and tossing her head.

I grasp her face and kiss it. I kiss Robert as he struggles to his feet, legs coated in sludge. Tears pour down my cheeks, and down his. I kiss him again and say against his mouth, "Thank you so much. Thank you for saving her."

He is gasping at the pain in his arm, but he holds me. He pushes his hands up through my hair and presses my face into his neck. He says, "I love you, Beatrice." We kiss, hasty, desperate kisses, then we remount and ride on towards Gewhorn Head.

After that we go more slowly. The wind is getting up and the sea smell is sharper, but land is near now. Suddenly there is grass under Saint Hilda's hooves, and the suck, suck of her footsteps turns to a dull beat. A high, tree-covered slope rises ahead. The moon vanishes behind a cloud. A dog howls, somewhere far distant to the north. I rein in Saint Hilda and we both dismount.

"Robert, you will need to find a way up through those trees, then go on north. Try to get to the monks at Cartmel. It's north and a little west of here. They'll help you, and see you on northwards. I have to get back fast now."

Robert stares at me. "Beatrice, you can't go back now. The tide's coming. You'll drown."

I wrap my arms round him. "Goodbye, Robert. I shall never forget you. God bless you." I kiss him and then jump back on to Saint Hilda. Robert grabs my shoulders and pulls me off again. My ankle twists in the stirrup and I cry out. He supports me with his shoulder under my arm, and frees my foot.

"Beatrice, don't be foolish. You'll never make it. Go

home later. Say I captured you. Or... come with me?" He sets me upright, holds me tightly, kisses me long and hard. I put my arms round his neck and press against him, return his kiss and stroke his hair, then I pull away and step back.

"Robert, don't you see, the choice has been taken away from us. If they find that I'm missing, nothing will stop them coming after you. If I'm at home, they will simply let you go."

"There was a choice, then?"

I climb back into the saddle, the man's saddle which Cedric put on my horse, and I wish I had my own more comfortable sidesaddle to help me travel faster. Robert is waiting for an answer, but I can't answer him. He seizes Saint Hilda's reins. "Listen, my darling, I don't mind having them after me, if you'll come. I'm afraid of what they'd do to you if they did catch us, but we have a good start. We can outrun them. With Saint Hilda, and maybe another horse at Cartmel, we can be in Scotland by the day after tomorrow."

I snatch the reins from his hands. "No. There are people who know the way better than we do. They know the short cuts. They'd cut us off. Get away, Robert. You have the chance to get away. Don't waste it. Don't waste all this." I turn Saint Hilda's head towards the bay. She bucks and shies. The smell of approaching salt, and of the bones of long-dead horses, is in her nostrils. I drum my heels on her exhausted sides. She skitters sideways, turns round several times as if trying to dislodge me. Robert attempts to catch her head, but I crack the loose end of the reins across her soft neck and whisper, "Come *on*, girl. Are you trying to kill all three of us?" Hearing my voice calms her, and at last she breaks into a grudging trot, heading back towards the sea.

"Beatrice!"

I look back. "Robert, go!"

Saint Hilda levels off into a tired canter and I do not look back again.

Chapter 22

As we reach the sands Saint Hilda almost seems to
know that we must follow the hoofprints of our
outward journey. There is no eelgrass path here – we must
have veered right away from it – but I scarcely need to
guide her head to follow our earlier tracks. The wind blows
harder and the moon is hidden behind cloud. Somehow or
other my lace cap has stayed on my head through all this,
but now the wind tears it off. My hair streams over my face,
and for a few seconds I cannot see. I hold it back with one
hand, and because for a moment I can feel Robert's hands
in my hair again, I almost turn back.

Half way across, the cloud shifts, buffeted by the tidal
wind, and a dazzling white light fills the bay. The far
headlands which I must reach look unfamiliar from this
side, and very distant. Then I see it, a flat, smooth ripple

of water moving in from the south-west.

In a frenzy I summon Saint Hilda's failing strength, but I know it is no good. The local measure of the tide's speed has always been 'faster than a galloping horse'. That's what they say when they warn children not to stray on to the sands. That's what they say when unfortunate travellers have been too slow. There can be no doubt. The sea will reach me before I reach the shore.

The oncoming wave is black-green, the colour of rot, of water-weed, of the mould on turnips when they cave in slackly as you touch them, the colour of death. The salt wind stings my eyes, and Saint Hilda finds new strength and thunders across the bay like an animal demented. The wave reaches us as I catch my first glimpse of the white chapel on the cliffs. Water sweeps beneath our feet, and I can no longer see the safe way to go. I head Saint Hilda in a straight line for the nearest point of the shore, and kick her into a flying gallop over the invisible sands. Spray flies up and soaks me. The wind rips at my hair and wraps it round my face. Seconds later, Saint Hilda falters. Her front legs give way. With a whinnying cry she buckles forward on to her neck. I crash over her head into the fast running tide. As I feel a gentle sucking at my limbs, I know that I have fallen in quicksand.

It is so cold. So dark. Icy water tasting like tears is in my mouth. Grit is in my eyes. At last the nightmare has me. I realise I have always known that it would, some day. The tales of childhood swathe me round and drag me down to their dead world. The sea is over my head. I have no sense of backward or forward, up or down. I cannot breathe. I have no knowledge of where to go for air.

A current is pulling me. In the midst of my choking, I sense that I have floated free. I thrash out with my arms, and my head breaks surface. Something more than a current is gripping me, a new terror. "Beatie, don't struggle!" The voice is indistinct but near. In a sudden shock, the warmth of night air slaps my clothes to my back, and I am out. Water is pouring off me. I am free of it. Everything is dark; sea and night are indistinguishable and I cannot clear my eyes and ears of them. Then, with a thump, the warm neck of a horse is under my face. It smells of stables, sun on meadows, things I never thought to see again. I struggle to sit upright, thinking I am on Saint Hilda, then realise that I am astride a much taller horse, and that a strong, pale hand is holding the reins. The horse staggers. My feet are trailing in water. They are pulled to the side by the force of the flow, my right foot dragged under the horse's belly.

"Slowly there, John! Follow me exactly," shouts a voice. Somewhere ahead a light flashes.

"Keep going! I'm behind you!" An arm is round me, gripping me. We zigzag, following the light. The sea is tugging at my thighs now. The voice ahead comes back faintly over the wind, "Firm ground ahead. Fast as you can! Head for the outcrop and the white chapel." Another horse becomes visible ahead as ours breaks into a futile attempt at a trot. Water surges up, splashes over my head again for a moment, and the horror returns. The animal's neck under my hands bulges and arches as it battles to move forward. Then suddenly my legs feel warm and naked. The horse surges forward, and we both lurch violently back. The splashing ceases, and the sound of the horse's hooves turns to a soft clucking noise underfoot.

In the white chapel they lay me on the cold stone floor. I am still choking out sea water from my mouth and nose. John Becker kneels down and wraps his cloak round me. "You might as well keep this one," he says. "You're wearing it more than I am." I try to stop gasping like a fish, but can't. I turn on my side away from him.

Eventually I ask, "Where's Saint Hilda?"

John props me with his arm. "Her neck was broken. She didn't get up again. I'm sorry."

"She was in quicksand. She would have drowned slowly." There is a terrible pain in my chest.

"No no no." John shakes me. "She didn't suffer. She was dead at once. Otherwise I'd have seen her struggle."

Cedric, by the window, looks at him, and John glances away, and I am amazed that this man who tells us all not to lie, should be prepared to lie for me. I let it pass. There was no choice in the end, and now I have to find a way to live with what I did. In that moment I think the pity of it might kill me. Robert is saved, perhaps, but at what a terrible price. I look at my life stretching ahead, purposeless and bare. I look at these two men who saved it. I say to them, hearing the emptiness in my own voice, "Thank you for coming to get me. You could have been drowned yourselves."

John stares up at the cobwebbed rafters. "I was afraid you were going to Scotland."

Cedric gives him a world-weary look, then turns back to the window. "Look!" He puts down his lanthorn and hauls me to my feet. Over the bay a shadowy moon is shining through torn clouds. Far off across the water, a light flashes, an uneven, jumping flame, a lighted branch perhaps. "There he goes." He passes the supporting of me to John, and raises his own lanthorn three times, so that the light of it fills the central window. It gusts and gutters as the wind catches it, flashing wildly its triple signal, the code for saved. "He knows you're safe, now. He'll get on northwards." Cedric looks at me for a moment. "Beatrice... if we find you dry clothes, and I take you across at tomorrow's low tide, you can still catch him at Cartmel."

I am starting to shiver. My teeth rattle in my head and salt water springs again from my eyes and nose. John holds me in an uncompromising grip, and the heat from his cloak and arms creates an air of steaming damp around us. "She's about to catch her death another way if we don't take her somewhere warm quickly," he says.

"We'll go home to the parsonage, Beatrice. Mother Bain will look after you and find you dry clothing. You're really going to have to stop wearing this red silk, you know, the trouble it gets you into."

I smile. I can't help it. Despite everything, despite all the reasons for not smiling, I smile, and he picks me up and carries me out of the chapel to where his horse is tethered under a tree. Cedric follows, and grasps my face in his fish-scented fist. "Beatrice, what is it to be? You have to make up your own mind."

John heaves me on to his horse. I look down at the Cockleshell Man. "Do you still want me to be your pupil, Master Cedric?"

He is silent, staring at me, then he says, "Aye, I do." He turns, and I see that he is limping. He reaches his own horse and calls back over his shoulder, "That's settled then."

Mother Bain is sitting in a high-backed wooden chair, in her nightclothes, smoking a small clay pipe full of juniper berries. "So, it's finished and done with, and we have all survived." Her voice emerges from under swathes of linen nightcap which all but hide her face. She chews the stem of her pipe. "And yet..." She shakes her head as if impatient with herself. "... no matter."

I am sitting on the opposite side of the parsonage's kitchen hearth, wrapped in blankets, sweating by the fire's fearsome blaze. Cedric and John are in dry clothes now.

All our drenched clothing is steaming on a clothes maiden near the ceiling, next to a row of dead grouse which are hanging upside down to cure. I am being forced to drink a disgusting brew of dandelion, lavender and hyssop, supposedly to cleanse the sea from my system. We are all being quiet, so as not to wake James who is asleep in the room behind the hearth, or Verity, asleep upstairs. Mother Bain gets up to tend Cedric's leg which was injured when he was whipped off his horse. John sits down in her place.

"We must get you back secretly to your room at the tower, Beatie. If your association with the Scot became known, you'd be an outcast. Even if you escaped retribution now, it would be held against you at the next raid."

I nod. I have given up bothering to speak, since it brings on my ague.

"They all know the Scot took a horse from Barrowbeck. They saw him go. So it is logical that Saint Hilda could be missing."

I turn my head away.

"You were in front of him on the horse, and it was dark. People who thought they saw someone with him were easily persuaded it was not so. There's no reason for anyone else to know you were ever missing. I'll take you to the edge of the clearing at dawn. If the watchmen see you, they'll probably just think you're up early. At worst they'll think you've been with Hugh."

I can feel a flush rising in my cheeks. "John..."

He goes on quickly. He doesn't want me to explain. I notice how weary and grimy he looks. His dark hair is still sticking in damp curls to his forehead. He brings a low stool and sits close to me. "I'm glad you decided to come back, Beatie."

I pull the blanket more tightly round me. He thinks Robert and I were lovers, and he doesn't care. I'm glad not to have to explain, because I don't know what I could say, how I could describe the strange and powerful bonding there was between Robert and me, feelings that are perhaps love's closest kin. If these past months have taught me nothing else, they have taught me that our enemies are much like us, after all.

A blackbird starts singing wildly outside the window, even though it is still dark. I look round at the leaping firelight, at Cedric from whom I am going to learn how to heal, at John who may one day be something more to me. Then I look towards the window for signs of a new day.